LUBIN
by
Danny White

CHAPTER ONE

WOLFPACK

The troop of schoolgirls walked noisily, as children invariably do, down the path that enters the green wood. High buzzing insect summer, butterflies flutter by and burning amber eyes follow the children as they invade the forest's green silence. They chatter on, unaware of the invisible watchers who note the white knee socks, the tartan skirts and the tasselled bonnets. They were supposed to be exploring nature in the forest, but their commotion drove all creatures into hiding.

In the heat of the day, the wolf pack pants in the cool bracken, preferring to sleep until the blazing sun reaches the far horizon. They lay and watch the girls as they return a few hours later, a little tired after their outing, a little more subdued and their neat clothing in some disarray. None of this interested the wolves as humans were to be avoided,

1

especially when in large numbers. At best, they grunt quietly and lick their fangs.

Others were also in the forest; two men who were marking the trees with white paint. The wolves were aware of them and the drug addict hiding with his deadly habit in bushes; also, there was a young man who had drank too much and was recovering in the cool shadows, oblivious to the world.

At last, the sun touched the horizon and the wolves yawned and stretched, brothers and sisters playfully teasing each other. Alphonse, the lead wolf growled and the play ceased as they sensed the air; in a short while, the twilight deer and twilight rabbits would appear to feed and the wolves must be in a downwind position to select their night's meal. The full moon provided some light through the canopy of leaves.

The wolves grey mottled fur now blended into the shadows apart from one; Tera was an almost albino with a lighter pelt than the others and her eyes were as blue as the day she was born. To the other wolves, even her mother, father, and siblings treated her as something special.

Alphonse froze and the others paused to wait for a further signal from him: something else was in the forest, something new to them, something confusing, and something to be feared. They sniffed at the air, opening their jaws to savour the multitude of scents over their tongues in the darkening gloom; eyes would be of little use here. All hackles were raised and bellies tight to the ground; ears flattened against the raised mane of their necks.

It dropped from the trees! Silently it pounced, a dark thing with fangs and claws larger and sharper than those that the wolves had. The whole creature was much larger and it's eyes were like the fires of hell; the screams and roars erupted as an ancient fury, it slashed and struck but the wolves were

For Ellie.

Mike Williamson with compliments

LUBIN

AND OTHER SHORT STORIES

Danny White
and
Mike Williamson

Danny White is a cousin of mine and also a brilliant artist, and the story of 'LUBIN' is his. Like me, he gets an idea in his head and he starts to paint, and in this case he also made up a story to go with the picture on the cover of this book, I simply filled in the blanks.

This is the second time we have worked together, as he produced the cover to my supernatural story 'OLD CHURCH' after reading the first chapter of the story which fired his imagination. The original painting is hanging in my home.

MW
Essex 2018

CONTENTS

alert and in their massed resistance from all quarters, the thing jumped at a tree and using clawed hands, it disappeared.

The wolves stood under the tree waiting for the creature to reappear, growling and snarling they circled the tree roots. They quickly realised that the danger was over, at least for the time being, and inspected each other. The only wolf that was damaged, a small nick on a paw, was Tera; she had been the nearest to it and the first to engage the monstrosity. Relieved that there were no other injuries, the wolves resumed their hunt for a midnight feast.

CHAPTER TWO

LEGEND OF LOUP-GAROU

"I tell you that I saw an albino wolf!" The young man who had been recovering from a hangover insisted to his friend as they drank morning coffee on a street café.

"I would believe you more if you said pink elephants!" His friend replied, "You were so hung over that you couldn't make out anything, and it was dark!"

"I heard this enormous dog-fight…"

"You just said it was wolves!" The friend laughed, "I told you that you are confused!"

"Perhaps he is not!" An old man had been listening to the argument, "There are stories of a wolf pack in the forest, and that at least one of them is an albino."

"There!" The recovering drunk slapped his friend on the shoulder.

"There are also stories of other things in the forest, far worse than a wolf and far older!" The old man added, "It would be wise not to enter the forest at night!"

The friend snorted, "Fairy stories! Old wives tales to frighten children!"

"It was my old wife that I lost to the wolves – or something more terrible!" The old man solemnly stared at them.

The friend felt uncomfortable under the old man's stare, "I am truly sorry to hear that and I meant no disrespect."

"I know you didn't," the old man said, "It is so easy to disregard stories as myths, or as you said, fairy stories. In all stories, there is an element of truth and in this case, there are wolves and other things in the forest."

"I am sure that there is," said the friend, "I was just having fun with him for drinking too much."

"He is fortunate," the old man said, "The wolves were out last night, I heard them, and there was something else hunting last night that could have found your friend."

Both young men did not know if to laugh or not.

CHAPTER THREE

THE MUTE GIRL

A month later, it was the school holidays and Teresa, Mona, and Christina from the school went for an early morning walk into the forest. All of the fresh foliage had burst out, the flowering trees had almost completed the bloom cycle and young fruits replaced them, testified by the song of humming bees.

While they were examining one patch of summer flowers, they heard a croak from deep in the bushes, a persistent croak and gasp. They cautiously ventured forward and saw that it was a naked girl, not much different to their ages. The girl appeared terrified of them and backed off, her croak louder than ever.

The girls made soft encouraging noises and slowly the naked girl calmed down and allowed them to approach her. Mona took out a plastic raincoat from her knapsack, and slowly draped it around the shivering shoulders.

"Poor thing!" Teresa said, "She is frightened; I wonder what happened to her."

Just then, they heard the cry of a wolf nearby. The girl became very excited and tried to pull away, but the girls held her tightly.

"That must be it," said Christina, "The wolves have frightened her!"

"Then what happened to her clothes?" said Mona. They asked but the girl became more agitated and croaked even more loudly.

"Why can't she speak?" Christina asked.

"Perhaps she can't, some sort of mute!" replied Mona.

With some difficulty, they dragged and coaxed the mute girl back to the village. Doctor Blanquer looked over his glasses at the bunch of girls bustling into his waiting room. His eyes popped open when he realised that one of them was dressed only in a raincoat.

"What have we here then?" he asked.

"Please Doctor, we found her naked in the forest," said Christina.

"And she can't talk, only croak," added Mona.

"Bring her into my office and I will examine her," Doctor Blanquer made way for them, "Now, I must ask you to stay in my office while I work."

The mute girl seemed terrified that the girls were leaving her and held onto Mona's arms very strongly. Seeing the girl's distress, the doctor allowed Mona to stay.

After a considerable time, Doctor Blanquer emerged from his office with a worried frown, "I can say that she is incredibly fit like a champion athlete, but her vocal cords have never properly formed, so she cannot speak. You would think that a pretty girl who must have had physical training, top quality at that, and cannot speak would be easily identified, and she has a birthmark on her right hand. Add to that is that you found her naked means that very probably, she comes from not too far away. Unfortunately, no one of her description has been reported missing."

"Do you know why she is so scared?" Christina asked.

Doctor Blanquer shook his head, "No idea at all, but she trusts Mona. The police will be coming here to take her photograph and then ask you to show them where she was found," he continued shaking his head, "Perfectly fit except for the voice!"

CHAPTER FOUR

LISA

The difference between Mona and the mute girl could not have been greater; Mona was dark with the glossy hair of a raven's wing and soft dark brown eyes, while the mute girl had very light blonde hair, almost white and eyes of bright blue. Mona's mother remarked on the difference when Mona brought the girl home. It had been decided that the girl could stay with Mona's family on a temporary basis.

The girl's nervousness was apparent; entering the house seemed to alarm her and it took some time for her to accept Mona's parents; her young brother Mark was strangely accepted. Wherever the girl had been appeared to have been very primitive, Mona had to show her how to use the bathroom and she ignored the bed at bedtime, preferring to curl up on the carpet.

At mealtimes, the girl ate with her fingers, and only when she was shown how to use the cutlery, did she clumsily use both the tools and her fingers. Mona's parents raised their eyebrows at this behaviour, "It looks as though she has been brought up by savages!" Mona's father said.

On the first morning, Christina and Teresa came round to the house out of curiosity. The mute girl and Mona were sitting at the kitchen table, the girl wearing some of Mona's clothes.

"She needs a name!" Mona said, "We can't keep calling her Girl or Hey!"

"We can try the usual names and see how she reacts," suggested Teresa. For an hour or more, they plied the girl with names, but all that the girl did was to hold her head to one side as though trying to understand.

"We can go on for ever!" sighed Teresa, "We should just pick a name and try to make her understand that it is her name."

"I agree," said Christina, "It's as though she never had a name!"

"Let me try something," Mona said. She pointed to herself and repeated her name several times, then she did the same with the other girls, then she pointed to the girl. Understanding flooded over the girl's face and then she growled.

At first, the girls were puzzled, and then Mona suddenly sat up, "That is her name! That growl is all she can say without proper vocal chords."

"We can't just growl every time!" Teresa objected.

"We choose a name, something short and simple," Mona decided, "then try to make her understand that is what we will call her."

"She is very pretty," said Christina, "it should be something that fits her appearance."

"Lisa!" said Teresa, "then we can have Mona Lisa!" and giggled.

"That is not such a bad idea!" Mona then said the name several times and pointed to the girl, and eventually the girl gave a soft growl. To confirm it,

Christina called the girl's new name and got an immediate response.

"The next task is to find her some clothes!" Teresa said.

"I think that the church has an assortment of clothes for the poor and needy," Christina said, "Try there first, and then we perhaps should buy something. How is your allowance?"

CHAPTER FIVE

FATHER RAMON

Father Ramon was surprised to find four young girls knocking on his door, but a short explanation of the predicament produced a smile on his round face.

"Of course, of course!" he burbled, "I have heard of the incident and this is the young lady in need of assistance. Welcome!"

"She can't talk," said Mona, "but we are calling her Lisa and she understands. She is very intelligent."

"A lovely name!" Father Ramon nodded his approval, "Come in and look at the clothes; some are in excellent condition with the labels still on."

Father Ramon left them too it and returned to his office. He rang several of his friends in other churches, hospitals, schools, and as an after-thought sports centres; anywhere the mute girl could have come from. Finally, he called the police to ask if they had any reports of a missing mute girl. No one had reported her missing.

He was troubled at the appearance of the girl; he had been at the parish for all of his adult life, slowly advancing to become a respected minister. During that time, he had heard all stories through the confessional as well as the usual grapevine, plus his predecessor collected a lot of history of the area, and one story stood out. It was about a young man who also could not speak, and was found naked and confused; the story ended with the premature death of the young man in a fire. He wanted to check the details, as it was so similar to this young girl.

At the same time as this young man, which was over one hundred years ago, there was a spate of sheep and cattle killings by a large predator. There were reports of a wolf-pack roaming the district and the killings were put down to the pack. He had recently heard that there had been some sheep lost in a nearby village and the wolf-pack was howling at the night. Last night, he had heard the wolves crying out, and that worried him. He took down a book from a bookcase and started to read; the title was *'Lycanthropy'*.

He read it quickly and replaced the book; then he went back to the girls. They had dressed Lisa in some new clothes and she appeared happy at that. He refused payment for the clothes and bid them farewell at the door; he watched them carefully as they went on their way, thoughtfully, he closed the door and went into the side chapel where he spent a long time praying.

CHAPTER SIX

SLAUGHTER

Farmer Girardin stood up with a sour and angry expression. At his feet, was the mutilated body of a sheep, and two more lay dead nearby. He looked round for signs of what had done this but all he could see was the dead sheep. It was obvious that a large dog had done this, or more probably the wolves that had been heard howling of late.

He lifted the bloodied bodies onto the trailer and drove back to his farmhouse, and from there he rang the police. He then, with his son Edward and a farmworker, he rounded up all of the sheep to bring them back to the sheds for the night; he brought in a few cows that he kept for milk as well.

As the twilight descended, the three armed themselves with rifles and drove out to the site of the slaughter; there, they met a similarly armed police officer. Girardin had prepared two of the dead sheep as bait, and they settled down to wait.

The night deepened and the sounds of humanity faded; the roar of distant traffic, the sounds of some television programme, a slammed door, and voices fading in the shadows. The full moon made it easy for the four guards to see every detail; the two dead sheep, the distant forest stood out as though it was daylight. In the distance, they heard a wolf baying at the moon, but it was a long way off.

In the shadows of the trees, Girardin saw some movement; something high up and not at ground level as expected. Wolves do not climb trees! His hand

14

tightened on the rifle and he saw that the others had seen the movement as well.

When it came, it came with the speed of a locomotive; a dark shape leapt from the trees and everyone fired. It was running towards the dead sheep, but now changed direction towards the new threat, the men! Girardin had time to notice the burning eyes before reloading and firing point-blank into the gaping jaws.

The dark figure appeared to explode; parts broke away, turned to black smoke and then black dust to fade among the shadows of the night.

Slowly, the men stood and walked towards the black mound of the creature, but it was no longer black, nor huge with burning eyes. Girardin gaped in astonishment and then horror as he realised that what lay on the ground was a naked young man!

The police officer spoke their thoughts, "We all saw something attacking the dead sheep and us; it was an animal of unknown species not this young man. What has happened?"

Girardin answered, "Not an unknown species, this is a wolf man, a werewolf, and when it died it returned to its original form."

"Surely you don't mean that!" the officer exclaimed.

"How else can you explain what has happened," the farmer answered, "It is either that or we are all guilty of murder!"

"And it's a full moon!" said Edward, pointing to the bright orb.

The farmer looked towards the forest and wondered; were all those old stories that his grandfather used to tell be true after all.

CHAPTER SEVEN

RUNAWAY

All night long, Mona had some problems with Lisa. The mute girl kept looking at the bedroom window and gave short sobs and whines. Mona wondered what was upsetting the girl; outside was a bright moonlit night, a night to sooth anxieties. Wondering if it was the bright moonlight that was bothering her, Mona went to the open window to draw the heavy curtains.

With a loud cry, Lisa bounded to the open window and leapt out! Mona stood petrified at the speed at which the act was committed; and then she looked out of the window expecting to see Lisa lying at least unconscious on the ground. Instead, there was Lisa running at high speed towards the fields and forest. Then, in the still bright air came the cry of a wolf.

CHAPTER EIGHT

JACQUES FORTIER

Jacques Fortier was the chief of police for the district. It was a comfortable position; nothing much happened in the quiet rural district and he could enjoy a full night's sleep and free weekends with his family. Today he was tending to his garden, his pride and joy.

He was only slightly annoyed when his other pride and joy called from the French windows, "Jacques, your office is calling you!"

With a quiet curse, he pulled off his gloves and threw them and the secateurs on the ground. He could not remember when he was ever called on a Sunday morning; he could smell the food cooking for a fine lunch.

"Yes, this is Fortier," he grunted down the telephone.

"Sorry to disturb you sir, but there is a report of a missing girl, ran off in the middle of the night!" the young officer on the telephone gave the impression of embarrassment and nervousness. The Sunday crew drew lots as to who would ring the chief.

Fortier snorted, "Ran away from her father, or ran away or off with her lover! What is special about this to other runaways?"

"She jumped from the bedroom window without hurting herself," The officer sounded relieved that the chief was not shouting, "The girl is a mute and found a month ago and since then we have been trying to find where she came from."

"Ah! I remember the notice," Fortier's voice softened; he had two daughters of his own, "We have found nothing since?"

"Not a thing and Father Ramon knows more of this that we do."

"I'm not surprised," Fortier gave a brief laugh, "If we ever need a bloodhound, I'll choose him! I'll go and see him before lunch, or maybe after," Mrs Fortier had been listening, and when she heard 'before lunch', her left eyebrow went up.

The meal was not as hurried, as Fortier realised that the church would be celebrating mass, and if he timed things correctly, he would meet Father Ramon in an empty church.

"You really should attend church more regularly," Ramon admonished when the officer arrived, "in any case, you can learn a lot from the chatter afterwards."

"And you have an advantage in the confessional!" Fortier replied.

"Did you ever meet my predecessor?"

"I never had the pleasure!"

"Johan Belcher, a good man but inclined to empty bottles!" Ramon smiled at the memory, "He never divulged anything from the confessions to anyone, but some evenings when there was just the two of us, he let things slip. Most of it was harmless but it did add colour to the character of the congregation!"

"That was long ago!" Fortier said, "What has that to do with the missing girl?"

"He left a written record," Ramon placed the hymn books on a shelf, "By rights, I should not let you read it, but it is also historical and he wrote about events long before his time; have you ever heard of Lycanthropy?"

"The word rings a bell, but I cannot recall it's meaning," Fortier said.

"It first appeared in Greek mythology; Zeus changed King Lycaon and his children into wolves, hence the name Lycanthropy, and about 50 AD in the *Satyricon* by Petronius in the time of Nero, but the legend goes back probably into the stoneage. It concerns loup-garou, otherwise known as werewolves!"

"Now you are confusing me!" Fortier said, "I am talking about a missing mute girl and you're talking about legendary monsters! Where's the connection?"

"It was the girl's speech or rather the lack of it," Ramon smiled and asked the officer to sit down, "Her speech consists of grunts, squeals and whines, exactly like my nephew's two Alsatians. It also reminded me of something that Belcher told me and I looked for it in his book; sure enough, there it is!" Ramon produced a small black book and opened it at a particular page, "Read that and I will make some coffee."

When Ramon returned, Fortier had read the few pages and laid the book down, "I still cannot see where you connect the two!"

"All of them had no speech to talk about, you did read that?" Ramon set the coffee down, "and when the creatures were killed, they reverted to their human form and were naked."

Fortier nodded, "I read that, but all of these were male, I read that there are no references to female werewolves!"

"There are in other references where females are called Lubins, and these are shyer than and not as aggressive as the male. As the male is more aggressive, they will be more obvious to us which we kill if possible."

"Are you telling me that the girl is a werewolf, a Lubin?" Fortier reached for the coffee and wished for something stronger.

"It is only a suggestion," Ramon settled down in his chair, "I have made exhaustive searches for this girl, where she comes from, without any success. I conclude from that either she dropped from the sky or has been here all of the time, under our noses!"

Fortier gulped his coffee and thought of what the priest was saying, "We have to search wider, perhaps she was on holiday and got separated from the group," he was desperate to find an alternative to Ramon's suggestion.

"In the summer, holiday groups come here from all over the world," Ramon pointed out, "schools arrange them, charter companies, historical groups, and then you have many families come here. I should imagine that it would take an enormous amount of time to locate all of these."

Fortier slumped; what the priest was saying was the truth, he did not have the resources to search the world for an unidentifiable girl, "There is another possibility; perhaps she was a prisoner, a sex slave and she escaped.

That would explain why there is no record of her and why no one has reported her disappearance to the police."

Ramon nodded, "That would also explain why she was naked."

"But you prefer the wolf idea!"

"There are reports of sheep being killed in the area, and wolves howling at night, that fits the wolf scenario." Ramon smiled at the officer.

"You haven't heard," Fortier took a deep breath, "There hasn't been time enough for the grapevine to react: in the early hours of this morning, three farmers and one of my men laid in wait for a sheep killer to appear. They fired on what they thought was a large dark predator, but it turned out to be a naked white young man!"

CHAPTER NINE

LISA RETURNS

A month later, Lisa reappeared very near the church. Again, she was naked and dirty, and confused. She was found at daylight by the church cleaner, Dorothy, who took her inside immediately and called out for Ramon.

"Oh dear, oh dear!" he exclaimed, "It is Lisa, but where has she been? Take her to the clothes and dress her, and try to clean her up. I'll inform the police."

Fortier was woken up, but when he realised the reason, he was out of bed and in the car within minutes. Ramon met him at the churchhouse door.

"Where is she?" the officer demanded.

"Calm down!" Ramon patted the man's chest, "You'll do yourself an injury and frighten the girl as well. She is eating in the kitchen, and I think that she remembers me and the church; that is why she came here, for help."

Fortier took a deep breath, "How can we help her? She cannot speak and I can't read minds!"

"She is quite intelligent, and I am sure we can work out some dialogue with her," Ramon led him towards the kitchen, "Have a coffee and be quiet and we may yet perform a minor miracle."

"I thought that she reacted well with that other girl, Mona something," Fortier took the coffee and stood in the corner while trying to not obviously look at Lisa.

"I had the same idea," Ramon nodded, "but it is very early and we should wait until the family wakes."

Lisa had not paused in eating in her usual style of mixing utensils and fingers, but she eyed the police officer and one could see that she was tensed to run at the slightest provocation.

After several cups of coffee, Fortier made for the door, "I'll go and get the other girl."

Lisa's reaction when Mona appeared was surprising; she ran up to Mona and started licking her face and making mewing noises. To stop her, Mona put her arms out and hugged the girl; after a hesitation, Lisa returned the hug.

"Can we keep her here?" Fortier asked quietly.

"It is obvious that she is a free spirit," Ramon answered, "and any attempt to control her will cause mental damage. I think that the friendship with Mona is as powerful as we can apply, and we hope that she feels a strong attraction to Mona and prefers to stay."

"I wasn't thinking of locking her up!" Fortier said, "She is very athletic and I think that any physical restraint will be a waste of time."

"Are you getting anywhere as to finding where she is from?" Ramon asked.

Fortier sighed, "We have spread our enquiries to the surrounding countries, but so far nothing at all. She is a real mystery and I am beginning to think of other possibilities."

"But you are dismissing the theory of the wolves!" said Ramon with a hint of a smile.

"There are no such things as werewolves!" the officer stated firmly.

CHAPTER TEN

KURT KRAMER

Kurt Kramer was on holiday; he had been on the same holiday for four years! He took a train from his home and travelled west until he saw a countryside he liked, and then he got off. After a reasonable period, he repeated the process again, and again.

He found a reasonable spot beside a hedge to pitch his small tent and looked at the scenery. On one side, he had a mountain descending towards the sea and on the other were fields of arable land and a village in the distance. This suited him fine; he would replenish his supplies in the village, and spend some time exploring the nature.

He lit the small gas fire and boiled some water for a cup of coffee. While he waited, he looked at the sun reflecting off the sea; the waves forming white maned sea-horses, the gulls wheeling high and he could hear their plaintive calling in the distance. He fell asleep before he could finish the coffee, while admiring the many glorious colours of the setting sun and listening to the song of the gulls.

Suddenly he came awake; perhaps it was the chill of the night air. He lay there for a few moments and admired the full moon. He heaved himself onto one arm and froze; facing him was a pair of brilliant blue eyes. He could not move as the wolf gazed at him, and then it leapt forward and licked his face, and the next moment it had vanished into the night.

To say he was astonished would be an understatement! He had anticipated having his throat ripped out but the lick on the face was almost as disturbing. Perhaps it was a tame wolf or at least one that was happy with humans. He made his way into the tent and his sleeping bag, resolving to solve that little mystery in the morning. As he drifted into sleep, the cry of a wolf baying at the moon filled the moonlit night.

In the morning, he packed up his gear and headed into the village. At the store, he enquired if anyone had a pet wolf; it just so happened that Fortier was buying his morning paper and overheard Kramer and his story of the meeting of a wolf in the night.

"There is a pack of wolves in the area," he informed the young wanderer, "I would advise you not to sleep outside as at least one of them is a killer; so far there have no reports of a human harmed, but there are a few sheep carcasses as evidence. Are you sure that it licked you?"

Kramer nodded, "I was really surprised, and when I think of it, it must have been looking at me for a few minutes. As far as I could see, there was just the one wolf."

Giving Kramer the address of a small hotel, Fortier walked down to the church.

CHAPTER ELEVEN

TWO MYSTERIES

"He is one lucky young man!" Ramon said when he heard the story.

"What do you make of his story?" Fortier asked, "I have never heard of a wolf licking a person, unless they were a meal!"

Ramon laughed, "Unless it was not a wolf! You should give some credence to the stories I tell you. The female werewolf, the Lubin is not the savage beast as the male. Perhaps we are dealing with one of those."

"What do you make of the blue eyes?" Fortier countered.

"Very attractive," Ramon's eyes twinkled with humour, "Dogs are born with blue eyes, but they change when they mature, except for a few that retain the blue eyes. There is nothing really exceptional in a canine having blue eyes."

Fortier grunted, "None the less, it is peculiar and also that it was a lone wolf, not the pack that we have been hearing about."

"It could have been an Alsatian," Ramon said, "They are remarkably similar, so perhaps he was mistaken."

"The same thought occurred to me," Fortier admitted, "so I checked all of the dog owners in the area; all accounted for and not one with blue eyes!"

"Surely that brings us back to a Lubin!" Ramon was laughing at the officer's expression.

"You will have me chasing legends and fairy stories!" the officer shook his head, "There is more to this than superstition!"

"Have you found out anything about the mute girl?" Ramon still had that mischievous gleam in his eye.

Fortier grunted, "That is a bigger mystery than your Lubin! We have checked far and wide but it looks as though she may be part of a large criminal action, possibly as a victim."

"A refugee, an illegal immigrant," Ramon grew serious, "Quite frankly, I hope that she turns out to be a Lubin rather than the misery that the girl may have gone through in the hands of some sick people!"

CHAPTER TWELVE
GIRARDIN DESCRIBES THAT NIGHT

The business with Farmer Girardin and the supposed werewolf was handled gently; it was decided that the young man who was shot was up to some mischief, or that he was mentally deranged as he was running around naked, so it was labelled as an accident.

Non-the-less, Girardin was highly upset, and understandably so as his own son was about the same age as the unfortunate youngster. He insisted that the funeral would be at his expense, but that was held up until the man could be identified. His rifle stood untouched in the corner of the kitchen where a spider had started to make a home.

The self-searching for reasons for the incident meant that eventually he would seek out spiritual help, and he found himself face to face with Father Ramon.

"I am convinced that I fired at a raging beast," he said.

"Tell me about the beast," Ramon asked as he sat the bewildered man down, "Tell me all that you remember however stupid that it may seem."

"I do not think that it was a wolf, or any other type of animal that I know," Girardin wrung his hands, "I think that it was in the tree tops, at least that was where we saw movement just before the attack; then it was there, running towards the sheep. It looked to me that it was as big as a rhinoceros and so black that it was difficult to make out any details; just a gaping jaw with the biggest fangs that you can imagine."

"What noise did it make?" Ramon asked.

"Something like a steam-whistle only louder; there was a deeper note like a lion's roar mixed with it. As it turned towards us, our first shots must have missed, I could see down its throat and the blood-red eyes as big as my fist or bigger."

"I would have been petrified with fear," Ramon said, "I would have been frozen to the spot; I'm surprised that you could react. What happened when you hit the creature?"

The farmer's face wrinkled with confusion, "It flew apart! We had just normal calibres but the only similar thing I have seen was with a large calibre rifle and explosive bullets."

"And you had normal ammunition?"

Girardin nodded, "There is no need for anything greater than we used."

Ramon leaned forward, "Describe what you mean by 'it flew apart'."

"I don't think that I can! Like a clay pigeon when it has direct hit, bits flew off and disappeared like dust or smoke. I'm sorry, but that is the best that I can do."

"That was excellent," said Ramon with a smile, "I have some old cognac and after that I think that you need some!"

"There is more!" Girardin stopped the priest, "I never told the police, but I could swear that as we approached the body it was covered with fur that melted away. The others are convinced it was a werewolf, but that can't be; it's an impossible legend!"

"I think that we both need that cognac!"

CHAPTER THIRTEEN

THE OTHER GIRL

Justine was a strange and lonely girl, but this was partly her fault. Her family had recently acquired a certain amount of comfortable wealth after centuries of the other extreme and with this Justine felt confused; she felt uncomfortable with the other children whose parents would refer to her as 'the other girl'.

In defence, Justine would put on the airs and graces of a princess, or at least what she thought was a princess. This of course annoyed everyone, including the adults. When she did this in school, there was often a punishment that she resented, and that reinforced her thoughts and actions.

She was shunned even by her parents; often overlooked and forgotten. In a quiet moment, she was sitting outside of the conditori when she heard a conversation, the sort of gossip that is frequently overheard in stores.

"They say that there was a young man shot nearby; I heard that the official verdict was accidental but I have also heard that he was killing sheep!" a middle-aged shopper said.

"No, you heard wrong! He was as naked as the day he was born and after some young maiden!" a younger woman said.

"I've heard that it was not a young man but a werewolf!" said a third woman.

"Don't be silly! You've been reading too many of those stupid magazines!" the first woman retorted.

"No, no! I have heard that there was a young girl found who could be a werewolf; perhaps we are surrounded by them and the young man was her male counterpart, and now she is after revenge!" the third woman said.

"I saw a stranger, a very blond girl over by the church, but I thought that they would not go in churches," said the second woman

"Or running water!"

Justine was intrigued; perhaps there was some truth in the gossip. She had noticed that the bothersome three, Christina, Teresa, and Mona with a new blonde girl, perhaps that was to what the gossips were referring; Justine had assumed that it was one of their cousins down for the holiday.

By the church, they had said, so Justine walked slowly and innocently down the street towards the church. Every Sunday, her family had taken their place in the pews, pretending piousness but the conversation at home showed that they were anything but! She took a seat in the corner, partially hidden by a pillar and waited.

Nothing happened that day, but Justine went home for dinner and returned for the evening mass. Father Ramon took a surprised second look as she entered the church; he knew her too well to suppose that she had a change of character.

At the end of the service, Justine lingered behind and approached the priest, "I understand that there is a new girl in town and wondered if I could help in any way."

Ramon was tempted to tell her that the best help was to stay away, "You mean Lisa! Yes, an unfortunate lost child that is staying with Mona's family for now, until we can find her family. Unfortunately, she is mute and that is proving to be a hurdle."

"Poor girl!" Justine feigned sympathy, "If there is anything I can do to help, please say so."

Ramon patted her arm, "Good of you to ask, but the police and other authorities are doing their best and Mona and her friends are providing ideal friendship."

"And there's always you and the church!" Justine said brightly. As she walked away, Ramon stood and looked at her; he knew of the girl's reputation and there was something wrong about the meeting, something uncomfortably wrong!

CHAPTER FOURTEEN

SOUND ADVICE

Kramer had decided to stay in the area for a little while; he was intrigued by the thought of a friendly wolf. He met Edward Girardin, the farmer's son, in a café and asked for a job and after meeting the farmer, it was agreed that he could work for at least the summer and stay in the guest-house. It could not have been better for the wanderer.

He ate with the family, and on the second evening, he told them of the meeting with the gentle wolf. There was total silence, even the knives and forks stopped moving. Edward slowly reached for the pepper-shaker.

"We have a wolf story, a recent one and not as pleasant an outcome as yours," he paused to sip some wine, "Something had been killing livestock, mainly our sheep, so we set up a trap and waited one night, four of us armed with rifles."

Farmer Girardin interrupted his son, "One of us was a police officer, or otherwise it could have been an even worse outcome!"

Edward continued, "The creature came out of the forest like lightning. It is difficult to describe what it looked like, what it was; it was huge, larger than a wolf and as black as sin, and when we fired, it sort of - flew apart. When we looked at the body, it was a naked young man. We know we fired at an unknown animal but we found no trace of another creature."

"I heard something in the village about a werewolf," Kramer said, "Is this what you are telling me about?"

Emptying his wine glass, Farmer Girardin nodded, "We were understandably all shocked, and the others are convinced that we had killed a werewolf. I do not believe in such matters!" he crossed himself

"The killings stopped immediately, and that convinced everyone that we had killed the werewolf," Edward looked at his father, "I am not sure what to believe!"

"It certainly does not match the wolf I met!" Kramer said.

"Probably yours was a real wolf, although I have never heard of one acting like that one!" Farmer Girardin said, and then resumed eating.

"It's the reason that I wanted to stay around here," Kramer explained, "The behaviour of that wolf was so out of character, that I want to meet it again."

Mrs Girardin, a quiet person whose eyes followed the conversation around the table, spoke for the first time, "You should be careful, next time, it could be a different wolf or not act so gently."

"I am sure that it is not violent!" Kramer said, "Somehow, it even looked different to the wolves I have seen before in zoos. Before it licked me, it had its head to one side as though asking a question as I have seen dogs do."

Edward laughed, "It was probably wondering what you tasted like!"

"Before you do anything rash," Mrs Girardin further advised, "you should speak to Father Ramon; he knows more about what is happening around here than anyone else."

CHAPTER FIFTEEN

A REVELATION

Mona, her brother Mark and the girls took Lisa for a walk through the village. The idea was to see how she reacted to what she saw in the stores, but it was another reaction that caused comment, one seen by Ramon and Fortier. There was small terrier being walked by its owner, a well-dressed, middle aged woman; when the terrier saw the girls, it went berserk, and then stopped barking and with a whine, hid behind the woman's legs.

Lisa had stepped away from the others and was staring at the terrier.

Mona frowned at her new friend, "The same thing happened to a cat the other day; it gave a great screech and hiss, and ran off."

"Look at Lisa's reaction!" Teresa said quietly.

The mute girl was standing like a statue, still staring at the terrier as the owner untangled the lead and dragged the still whining dog away.

"It's just a daft dog!" Mark said.

Mona said nothing but took Lisa's arm and pulled her towards a store window. The rest of their walk was uneventful.

The priest and officer were on opposite sides of the street, and they walked towards each other. "What do you make of that?" said Fortier.

"All I can say is 'interesting'," Ramon rubbed his chin, "I hate to say it, but it is what I would expect with a werewolf."

"She didn't attack the dog!" Fortier objected.

"Ah, but are we talking about a werewolf or a less aggressive Lubin?"

"There you go again," Fortier snorted, "trying to put ideas into my head!"

"You must have thought something about the theory," Ramon nudged his companion's arm, "C'mon, admit that you have!"

Fortier gave a huge sigh, "Yes I have, and I must remind you that it is my duty to consider every possibility however strange it would appear."

"Very Maigret or Sherlock of you!" Ramon smiled at his small victory.

"Next, you will be telling me that it is huge dog on the Moors!" Fortier accepted the reference to the famous fictional detectives, especially Maigret.

"Not really," Ramon said, "Have you thought about what you shall do if a werewolf or a Lubin is involved?"

"Since I don't really believe in it, the answer is no!" He really had not thought that far ahead.

"It is a double problem," Ramon held up one finger, "If it is a werewolf, you should try to kill or subdue it before it attacks you," he held up a second finger, "However, if it is a Lubin, there may be no need to kill the creature."

"How can you tell the difference?" Fortier scratched his head.

"That is for you to solve," Father Ramon said, "But I would think about it before it surprises you!"

CHAPTER SIXTEEN

THE ARTIST

Mona's home was the last house in the street, beyond the garden boundary were the enticing fields and forests. For Mona's brother Mark, it was heaven! He spent most of his time studying nature, and he had his father's old camera to record things that he saw as he meandered over field and forest. He had also developed a skill with a pencil, and with a pad balanced on his knee, he would make fine sketches that he later used to create water-coloured paintings.

This day, he was perched on a fence looking towards the forest when Mona and Lisa arrived. The mute Lisa looked over his shoulder and became very interested, whimpering and jabbing her finger at the drawing and then pointing excitedly at the forest.

"She understands what you are doing!" Mona said, "I think that it is the first time she has seen artwork."

"That is strange!" Mark frowned, "How can you go through even a few short years without seeing art?"

Lisa was trying to take Mark's pencil away; Mark turned to a fresh page in his sketch book and gave her the pencil. Her first attempts were clumsy but within minutes, she had drawn the recognisable head of a deer. She pointed again at the forest and two deer emerged.

"She has a better eyesight than me!" said Mark, "I couldn't see them!"

"I couldn't either," Mona looked at the girl thoughtfully.

"If this is the first time she has used a pencil and has never seen art before, she has remarkable talent." Mark took the pencil back.

"I think that she should meet Maria!" Mona said, "She will know what to do with her."

"The art teacher?" Mark nodded as Lisa tried to understand what they were saying, "That is a good idea, we will go now!" he continued.

Marie Becaud was an odd sort of person who lived in a small old house near the centre of the village, not far from the school. As far as she was concerned, nothing existed outside of art, any art, painting, literature, and music; as the children approached the house they could hear classical music being played very loud.

They knew better than to knock on the door; their knocking would not have been heard above the music, so they walked to the back where Maria worked in a conservatory. At first, they could not see her but then a plume of blue smoke drifted above a canvas on an easel. She was not surprised to see them as children often came around to see her working; she even managed a smile around the dark cheroot stuck between her teeth.

"Hi kidos! What can I do for you today?" She reduced the volume of the music.

Mark stepped forward, holding out the sketch book with Lisa's drawing, "What do you think of this as a first attempt?"

Maria took the book and studied the drawing over her bifocal glasses. For some minutes she looked closely before handing back the book, "Who drew it?"

Mark pulled Lisa forward; she had been staring with amazement at all of the paintings untidily placed around the conservatory, "This is Lisa and she is a mute. When she saw me sketching she became very excited and so I let her do that drawing of a deer and from what we can understand, it is the first time she has seen a work of art."

Maria nodded, "I have heard of her! Come here child!" She held out her hands and Lisa stepped forward. Maria examined the girl's hands, "Powerful hands with peculiar narrow nails!"

Lisa demurely allowed the artist to examine her, even to the extent of Maria stroking her face. The artist abruptly turned away but held Lisa's hand. She scrabbled on a bench, found some charcoal, and then led the girl to a pad of blank paper. Quickly she outlined a face that could have been Mona's face and then gave the charcoal to Lisa, gesturing towards a clean sheet of paper. Hesitatingly, Lisa started to draw a head and it was unmistakably that of Maria.

"If this is the first time she has done art, she is a natural!" Maria said softly, "We are in the presence of genius!"

"That's what we thought and brought her to you," Mark said, "Now what shall we do?"

"Go into the kitchen and you will find some lemonade and a stale cake," Maria was already preparing for the next stage, "You can sit around, read a book, or whatever, Lisa and I have some serious work to do!"

Maria removed the canvas she was working on and replaced it with a smaller fresh canvas. Quickly she drew an outline and then started to add oil colours with Lisa looking on intently. It was a bouquet of roses done quickly in the impressionist style. Propping up the wet painting so that it could be seen, Maria turned to Lisa and held out a brush; the invitation was obvious and Maria lit another cheroot and stood looking at the girl's handiwork.

"The wonderful thing about teaching is coming across a pupil as good as this!" Maria puffed out her blue smoke, "It does not happen often, probably once in a lifetime but when it does, the feeling is transcendental!"

CHAPTER SEVENTEEN

JUSTINE HAS A FRIGHT

Father Ramon watched from a distance as the children walked through the village; he saw them enter the artist's house and emerge sometime later with some sheets of art paper. He saw them as they went to each of their houses, or shopping in the store; he noted the reaction from animals and even some people to the strange, attractive mute girl. He noted with some discomfort that the rebellious Justine followed many times at some distance; he was sure that it was no coincidence that she was going the same direction.

Lisa had taken to sketching in coloured pencils, and one evening she was sitting on the fence and looking at the lengthening shadows as she quickly captured the changing scene on paper. In the shadows behind her, Justine moved quietly to steal up and see what the mute girl was doing. "Drawing pretty pictures are you?"

Startled, Lisa whirled round, dropping the pencils and pad to the ground; a growl came to her throat and her hands became hooked claws.

Surprised at the violent look in Lisa's eyes which had turned green, Justine backed up a little, "So you are a wolf-girl just as they said in the village!"

The resulting snarl came from behind her, and with a terrified look she saw five full grown wolves; they were creeping closer with their lips pulled back to expose gleaming fangs. Panicking now, she moved towards Lisa who gave a soft growl; the wolves stopped moving but continued snarling. Caught between two violent looking alternatives, Justine gave a great cry and ran towards the centre of the village, straight into Father Ramon and Kramer.

"What's wrong girl?" Ramon said as he held her arms.

She stuttered so badly that they had trouble understanding her, but eventually she pointed backwards and said, "Wolves!"

Kramer took off at great speed in that direction. When he got to the fence, he saw Lisa crouching on the ground, "Are you alright?"

Lisa quickly stood up and whirled around, and for a split-second, he could swear that he saw grey shadows moving away from them. Lisa smiled which distracted him.

Kramer picked up the pad and pencils and took her hand, "Come on, Father Ramon is probably waiting for us."

Ramon was still holding on to a hysterical Justine and as Kramer and Lisa appeared, she pointed, "She's a wolf! I saw her with wolves and they threatened me, they were going to kill me!"

Ramon shook her rather more roughly than he intended, but he was sure she was up to no good, "That is nonsense! How can she be a wolf? Think of it; who has fed you this nonsense?"

"The whole village is saying so, and I saw her!" Justine screamed. She was creating such a fuss that windows and doors were flung open as people enquired as to the cause of the disturbance.

"Kramer, take the girl home and I will attend to Justine," Ramon instructed, he wanted to get Lisa away from the attention the commotion was bringing. Unfortunately, it was too late; Jacque Fortier intercepted them before Ramon could arrive at the church.

"What's going on?" he demanded.

"That – that thing is a wolf!" screamed Justine.

"What thing?"

"She is referring to Lisa, the mute girl!" Ramon ushered them both through the church door.

"Not that nonsense again!" Fortier snorted.

"There was a pack of them with her and they tried to attack me," Justine collapsed on the floor in tears.

Fortier looked at Ramon who shrugged, "I told that fellow Kramer to take Lisa home, and I did not see or hear wolves or any dogs."

The police officer looked down at the weeping girl, "Something upset her, that's for sure. Kramer took the girl home?" Ramon nodded. "Then I will go there now," Fortier jammed his hat on his head and walked away.

As he closed the door, Justine screamed at him, "She should be shot like all beasts!"

CHAPTER EIGHTEEN

THE INTERVIEW

"Can a wolf do that?" Mona's father pushed a drawing under Fortier's nose.

"I am not the one who is calling the girl a wolf! I think that it is ridiculous, but something has upset this other girl and I am duty-bound to investigate." Fortier took the drawing and held it at arm's length, "I am no expert, but I am sure that a wolf cannot do anything like this."

"Marie Becaud said that Lisa has a natural talent," Mark said, "She is planning an exhibition of Lisa's work."

"Where is the girl now?" Fortier handed the paper back.

"Upstairs with Mona," Mona's father said, "She is extremely upset and we may have to call the doctor. She can't answer any of your questions anyway, waste of time."

"So no one was with her at the time, none of you?" Fortier picked up his hat, "Just you Kramer."

"No, I ran there after that lunatic came running at Father Ramon and me, as far as I could see, Lisa was totally alone," Kramer replied, "if there were wolves, she would have been killed, so it must be nonsense!"

Slowly he walked back to the church, thinking through all that he knew and occasionally shaking his head in frustration. Justine was still there, only now sitting in a pew, with Ramon talking to her.

"What were you doing in that garden? It is private property and you are not known to be a friend of Mona or the other girls." Ramon said.

"I wasn't thinking about where I was going," Justine squirmed in the seat, "Anyhow, it was dark!"

Ramon shook his head, "It was light enough for Lisa to draw the scenery."

"That bitch! Don't you know that wolves can see in the dark?" Justine spat out.

"She is not a wolf!" Ramon sounded angry, "You are sitting in God's house and committing sins; first you lie about what you were doing there, you have been seen following her, and second, you are saying that there are such things as werewolves; that is the Devil's tongue that you have. You have too much anger in you for such a young person."

"So you have been following that girl?" Fortier entered the conversation, "Why would that be?"

"I can walk where I want!" Justine flared back.

"That is not strictly true," Fortier corrected her, "It rather depends on the reason for being there in the first place. If your intentions were not good, you could be in a lot of trouble, more than you could imagine, and as for telling falsehoods about someone, that can be easily proved and cause more trouble for you."

Justine bit her lip so hard that blood spurted down her dress. Ramon immediately brought out a handkerchief, but Justine pushed it away, "It's not fair! Those girls get all of the good things, and then that new – girl gets even more!"

"The fault could be yours!" Ramon talked gently now, "Think about it, if you are unpleasant, people will be unpleasant to you in return." Justine said nothing and Ramon cleaned the blood from her face.

"I am going to leave this in your hands Father," Fortier said, "I'll look around at first light but I do not think we'll find anything."

CHAPTER NINETEEN

THE LUBIN

The story of Justine's encounter with the wolves circulated very quickly, and people crossed the road when seeing Lisa and her friends; the also crossed themselves like any good Christian. Mona was usually a good tempered girl but the attitude and stupidity of the villagers made her see red.

"How can they believe that she is a wolf?" Mona exploded one day, "She is gentle and kind, and she is artistic; I have never heard of a kind, artistic wolf!"

Jacques Fortier was standing nearby, "Superstitions are difficult to overcome. We had them long before Christianity."

Father Ramon was with the police officer, "Yes we did, and some people think that Christianity is also superstition. In troubled times, people revert to their beliefs and those primitive beliefs are very strong, incredibly strong."

"What troubles are we having now?" Mona asked.

"The story of the werewolf that Girardin claims to have shot is a threat to our existence, our way of life and beliefs, and the conflict makes them nervous." Ramon explained.

"They actually believe that people can turn into animals!" Mona said, pulling a face.

"People can be very strange," Fortier nodded, "I do not believe in such things, but there have been some peculiar things happening of late."

"Where is she now?" Ramon asked.

"With Marie Becaud," Mona replied, "They get along together very well, and you should see the paintings that Lisa is doing now! Marie is very impressed."

"I think that I will go and see for myself," Ramon said, "will you becoming with me?"

Fortier shook his head, but Mona jumped up, "I'll come with you."

They could hear the loud music before they saw the house. Ramon and Mona stood in the doorway and watched a remarkable scene; Marie and Lisa were dancing wildly, Marie with a glass of wine in her hand. When the visitors were noticed, they stopped dancing and broke down in a fit of giggles; Lisa had a peculiar rough giggle, almost barking or whining.

"I came to see the artwork, not someone dancing!" Ramon said with a huge smile.

Marie took a deep breath, "All art is the same! A painting can inspire a piece of music, and both can inspire the written word, and vice-versa. It is the creation that counts."

Ramon clapped his hands, "Bravo! A celebration of life, I couldn't agree more."

Marie took a drink from the glass and eyed the priest, "It could also mark the opposite. Don't you think that we should also celebrate the passing of one soul to another existence?"

"We do, although with more modesty," Ramon smiled.

"Where are the paintings that Lisa has done?" Mona bounded forward to look at a canvas on an easel, "Oh!" She was obviously surprised.

Ramon came and stood next to her, "Excellent work and a surprising composition."

The picture was of Lisa next to a blue eyed wolf, just the heads with the full moon behind them.

"I didn't do a thing to help her," Marie said as she lit a cheroot, "The strange thing was that I was teaching her to do a self-portrait, and she drew the wolf's head; only after that was complete did she draw the girl's head."

"Perhaps she has heard all of the gossip about the wolves," Mona suggested.

"Perhaps," said Marie, "perhaps."

Lisa looked from one to the other, trying to follow the thoughts. She waved her hands and stood next to the painting; obviously, she was asking for a comment.

Ramon took her hand and patted it, "Very good, excellent workmanship!" Lisa smiled and hugged the priest.

They stayed a while and looked at all of the work done by Lisa; it was an enormous amount.

"I had to fetch more material," Marie informed them, "and I am expecting someone from Paris soon to arrange an exhibition."

They were all impressed, "Fancy that!" said Ramon.

As Mona and Ramon left, it was Mona who spoke their thoughts, "It was as though she was telling us a story, and that she is a werewolf."

"Or it could be as you suggested earlier, that she heard the stories from the village," Ramon tried to make an alternative answer, "If she is as you said, she would be a Lubin not a werewolf."

"What is a Lubin?"

"A female werewolf," Ramon explained, "They are shyer than the male and a lot more gentle."

"That could describe Lisa!" Mona gasped.

"I am aware of that, but for the time being I do not want to mention it to anyone," Ramon grasped her arm, "You must not mention it either, for her sake."

CHAPTER TWENTY

TERA

Summer was almost over, and the question of school arose; what could they do with Lisa? Apart from her disability to talk, there was also a problem with the attitudes of the other children and teachers. If anything, the gossip had become worse and when they walked through the village, there were hostile glares and muttering from almost everyone.

A man came from Paris, Charles Breton, a well-dressed man of average height and very excitable, especially when he saw Lisa's paintings. Mona, Lisa, Christina, Teresa, and Ramon, told Lisa's story, as far as it was known but avoided any mention of wolves.

Breton's eyes shone, almost watered, as they spoke and he looked at Lisa, "This is even more wonderful! A brilliant artist and mysterious as well. I think that she will become a very famous young artist."

"That is what we are hoping," Ramon said, "If she becomes famous, perhaps someone will recognise her and we will find out her history, where her parents are."

"Ah, yes!" Breton nodded, "That would also add to the allure, the solving of the riddle."

Breton drove away, and everyone looked at one another, but no one said anything.

It was decided that Lisa's education could wait a while, until her story was flashed through the media. She spent the time painting with Marie and wandering through the fields and forests. Sometimes Mark would be with her as they both took the sketch pads.

On the second week of the school term, Mona came home to find Lisa in an agitated mood; she was restless and making small noises. She dragged Mona outside and pointed to the forest. They quickly ran over the field and entered the dark shadows.

Lisa signalled that Mona should stay as she stepped forward. Suddenly, Mona was aware that she was surrounded by wolves, but they were relaxed and not threatening in any way. Lisa appeared to be communicating with them, and as she grunted and whined, she began to change shape.

Mona looked on in amazement; her friend's jaw began to jut forward along with the nose, her ears enlarged and became furry points, and her hair vanished to transform into a wolf's mane. She turned towards Mona, and her hands, those wonderful artistic hands, were now claws.

Dropping on all fours, she wriggled out of the clothing and came up to Mona; she laid her head on Mona's lap. The other wolves stood and waited, as with tears, Mona said her goodbye. She had always known in her subconscious that Lisa was a Lubin, a female werewolf, and that the time would come when they would part company.

With a final lick of Mona's hands and tear-stained cheek, the Lubin Tera turned and ran off with her true family. Later that night, as a gentle breeze wafted the bedroom curtains and spread the bright light from a full moon, the cry of the wolf could be heard across the fields and meadows. Was it hallo or a goodbye?

THE END

TIME RETURNED

It was a typical evening on the small tree lined cobbled street; the leaves were still the bright young green of spring. The air was cool in the shade after the heat of the afternoon, and the couple walked hand in hand, passing other couples and young children unnoticed. Occasionally, they stopped and sat on a bench, always holding hands, looking only at each other with the intensity that only young people do. These lovers had hair the colour of shining snow.

There is nothing in any rule book that says that only the young can possess great passion, as exhibited by this old couple. Their skin was paper dry and their faces lined, but they glowed as though the setting sun reflected there.

When did they first meet? Was it today as they passed the artist's stalls by the river, the paper and canvas bright with coloured dreams, or yesterday when her hair was a golden halo and his step was firm? Perhaps her hair was like a raven's wing, shiny and glossed in a myriad of sparkling black strands; it is hard to tell now. Her companion was still the brave young man of yesteryear to her as she stared across their hands in bond; the neat moustache neatly trimmed and the smile revealing strong white teeth.

While they sat and gazed into each other's eyes, the sun stopped on the horizon, trembled, and as they sat like statues, the shadows reversed, the evening became midday when they had lunch, and then glorious morning, followed by snowflakes drifting unnoticed to settle on their hands and faces. After a while, the leaves turned red and yellow, falling from the trees to colour the autumn grass and then it was summer, an old summer of their youth, full of dreams of fire and promise.

Gradually, as the years unwound, her hair took on the glow and shimmer of starlight; his faded eyes became again a fierce summer blue, his hands were strong and gentle, caressing the softness of a girl's skin. Her young smile was full of the sweetness of red fruit, cherries and strawberries.

From somewhere, probably in the market, he had plucked a white flower, a gardenia and this he placed in her hair. They rise hand in hand as the sun set, and the new moon shone on the perpetual lovers as they walked once more into a life that was familiar and real to them, seen once to be relived in a future time.

THE END

A STRANGE CAPTIVITY

CHAPTER ONE

BISHOPMOUNT

It was well past the devil's hour, and a palpable silence reigned. The few street lamps provided pools of soft orange light in the darkness, giving light for a grey cat that walked under a lamp to sit and wait for some feline affair.

Faint shadows like mist or hot breath drifts through the scene and the grey cat looks at them intently; what she sees there soon fades and then she looks away. The thoughts in that elegant head are alien to normal humans, and as there is nothing else of interest, she slowly saunters into the shrubbery in someone's front garden.

Just as the first pale signs of morning began to show in the sky, Martin Benyan began to deliver the milk to his customers. He was raised in the old traditions, shunning the use of a motor vehicle, even an electric one, and he had Old Moses, a brown pony to haul a light cart that jingled with the movement of glass bottles and the shiny brass and leather harness. Apart from the clip-clop of Old Moses' hooves, the jingle of bottles like wind-chimes was the only sounds in the morning.

Christine Hannan loved the old world sound as she lay in bed, slowly wakening with the clip-clop rhythm to a new day, and she knew that shortly the melodic song of the blackbird would herald another dawn. Her hound Jamie, of uncertain age and even more unknown parentage, would wait until he was sure that she was awake and then jump on the bed to make a fuss.

In a small village of Bishopmount, like many others in Suffolk and beyond, life progressed slowly, imitating the pace of Old Moses. On the village green, they played cricket in the summer, and retired to the Wooley Shepherds Arms public house at the end of play, frequently joining the Morris Dancers who performed on the forecourt. If cricket was too energetic, there was always the crown green bowling club behind the pub.

Opposite the pub, across the green, was St Botulph's Church and next to that was the rectory, the home of Roland Thurber who was known to join the revellers at the end of play. Roland was almost of pensionable age, not that he was thinking of stepping down; he had been in the village far too long to contemplate such action.

The church was also of a great age, possibly erected in the 9th century on the site of another building; it was almost invisible behind a curtain of yew trees. The village of Bishopmount was even older than that; in Suffolk, any rise in the land, however trivial, is considered a hill, hence the name. When the land was always flooded centuries ago, the mount became an island and claimed by the Ancient Britons as an easily defended residence. The testament for this is a low and almost invisible ruin, just a few stones indicating that walls once stood there in times that are more recent.

With the arrival of the milk, breakfasts were prepared and eaten to be shortly followed by the noise of engines, as first, the workers left and then the school bus arrived to transport the older children to

Felixstowe. There was a small nursery school for the younger children next to the church.

Then almost silence. Perhaps there was the muted sound of a radio playing morning music, and the sound of water as the breakfast plates and cups were washed and put away.

It was as though the whole village had departed, vanished with the coming of the sun like the night-time shadows. This dream-state was broken as the single village store-cum-post office owned by George Sommers was invaded by the housewives, who stopped, chatted, and met in each other's house for morning gossip coffee. Bicycles squeaked for lack of oil as they slowly passed over the cobbled streets and the more industrious laboured over their roses and petunias.

In the late afternoon, it was as though a film was run backwards as the school bus arrived and deposited the children, followed by the roar of engines as the workers arrived home and meals were cooked and eaten.

Children then went to play, filling the village with the sounds of laughter and screams. Men, the owners of various dogs would take them for a walk that inevitably ended at the Wooley Shepherds Arms. Tall tales were told and plans made, while some played darts and dominoes.

Nothing could be more normal as an Olde World English village like Bishopmount - that is until an evening in late May.

As the customers left the Wooley Shepherds Arms, the sky lit up as though there was a great lightning storm, but no sound was heard and no forked lightning to be seen; the light was a bright blue green that lasted for about five minutes, as though the green spring grass had been transferred into the heavens. A crowd gathered outside the pub and looked around for the cause; not a cloud was in the sky and the stars somehow managed to twinkle back at them through the light.

The Reverend Thurber was among the crowd, "Just some static electricity I wouldn't wonder," he surmised and everyone dismissed the incident, but more was to follow.

The pub proprietor, Trevor Watts stayed out after the others had gone home. Prior to being a landlord, he had been an electrical engineer and what had happened was not like anything he had seen or heard of before; electrical discharges came and went in a blink of an eye and not hang around for minutes. He was quite sure that the phenomenon was nothing to do with static electricity.

CHAPTER TWO

A NEWCOMER

Christine woke at the sound of hooves but it was still pitch black. Puzzled, she looked at the time and saw that it was not quite three, too early for Martin to deliver milk. Curious as to what was making the noise, she left the warmth and comfort of the bed and a startled hound, drew back the curtain and peeked out of the window; coming down the street was an old fashioned Romany caravan pulled by a dark horse. All that she could see of the driver was a pair of sunburned hands holding the reins as it passed through the orange light of a street lamp.

She watched as it passed by and wondered where it had come from and where it was going; the old Romany caravans were rarely seen these days. When the caravan passed out of sight, Christine returned to her bed and slept for a few more hours.

The other villagers had also seen and heard the caravan, and this was the main conversation in the village store; they were so eager to discuss their opinions about the caravan and its occupant that the store quickly filled with the babble of voices.

Mrs Victoria Wright, a tall thin well-dressed woman spoke the loudest, "I hope that this does not mean that we will be invaded by those creatures; every time they arrive the crime level goes up!"

"It may have been just passing through and will be someone else's problem," Miss Julia Probert, a short stout woman said.

The store owner George Sommers smiled at the women; he was politely waiting for a pause in the chatter so that he could sell something, but there was no immediate pause.

Slowly, the conversations stopped one by one and he sold some bread and some postage stamps. The store emptied, and he sighed with relief. He started to arrange items in the store, but half an hour later, the bell on the front door rang; he looked up to see a stranger looking round the shop.

"Good morning sir, can I help you?" he enquired.

"Want something for breakfast," the stranger replied. He wore a dark grey peaked cap and an old dark jacket that had seen better days, but the most compelling feature was bright green eyes peering out of the much sunburned face.

"We have some bread and cereals, and there is a batch of fresh rolls made by my good lady. Would you want some tea, coffee, milk, Mister...?" George guessed that this was the Romany traveller that caused the gossip.

"Ambrose, Jack Ambrose, and I'm stopping for a few days before moving on. Do you have any bacon and a few eggs?"

"Yes we have!" George led the way to a cold cabinet, "We have some meat pies as well. Was that your caravan that came through this morning? Don't see many of those these days."

"Yes it was!" Ambrose nodded, "Can't abide those motor things, and I'm in no rush to go anywhere. I'll have some backy as well."

"You're welcome here anytime," George took the money and gave back some change. For some reason, George did not think that Ambrose was the normal sort of Romany.

CHAPTER THREE

AMBROSE

It was two boys, Georgie and Sam, playing hooky from school and fishing without a licence, who saw the smoke from Ambrose's fire rising above the trees. They crept through the bushes to see what it was and saw the Romany caravan for the first time, although they had heard the gossip.

They were fascinated by the bright colours and patterns and the horse quietly grazing nearby. Ambrose appeared and poured some coffee from a tin next to the fire into a mug. He settled down on a stool and lit a pipe. The two columns of smoke, one from the fire and the other from the pipe, joined towards the sky.

The boys were in a quandary; if they told what they had seen, they would reveal what they were doing. As they thought about this, Ambrose disappeared and in a few minutes was standing behind them, his pipe clenched in his teeth.

"Not nice to spy on folk!" he said gruffly. From the boy's vantage point on the ground, Ambrose looked as tall as the trees.

"We, - we weren't spying sir," said Georgie, "we saw the smoke and wondered what it was."

"Well, now you know," Ambrose blew a smoke ring, and the boys watched it drift away in amazement, "Shouldn't you be in school?"

The boys looked down at their shoes without saying anything.

"We can have a deal," said Ambrose, "I won't say anything about you, if you say nothing about me! Deal?" The boys nodded.

There is no such thing as a secret, not really, so a few days later, Christine ran after Jamie who had followed his nose into Ambrose's camp.

"Oh, I am sorry," she blushed prettily, "Jamie is such a scamp!"

Ambrose bent down and patted the dog, "He has a bit of everything in him, mostly a spaniel. Nice Jamie!"

Christine walked forward to attach the lead to the dog's collar, but Ambrose stopped her. "Let him run; he won't do any harm. Stop a while and have some tea, it's a bit strong!"

"My dog likes your caravan, something new for him." Jamie was sniffing excitedly around the caravan, "I saw you arrive a few days ago, in the middle of the night!" she said. Jamie backed away with a growl from the dark horse.

"I like to travel when it is quiet," he replied.

So Christine stopped and chatted, finding out that this 'Romany' was very well educated and as he talked the country accent disappeared. The time passed, and with a start, Christine jumped up.

"I am sorry!" she said, "I meant only to take Jamie for a run and I have so much to do."

"You're welcome to call again, and bring Jamie; it's been a pleasure!" Ambrose watched her walk away.

"What do you think of that?" he said quietly, and the answer was a mumble from behind the wagon.

It was Christine that informed the village of the whereabouts of the 'Romany' Ambrose. That started another round of gossip in the store and around the afternoon tea parties.

CHAPTER FOUR

ROLAND THURBER

The Reverend Roland Thurber thought seriously about the green flash. He was interested as any natural or unnatural occurrence was ultimately associated with God. Although he had dismissed the event at the time, that was just to still any alarm that the villagers would feel.

He looked up on the internet what could have caused the event, and was surprised to find that recent research had revealed that the magnetic field of the planet was responsible for a number of strange phenomena. The Earth's atmosphere acting as a lens or crystal to separate out the different wavelengths of light could cause peculiar effects; green light was especially mentioned and many peculiar observations had no explanation at all.

One thing that he noticed was that most of the phenomena were at sunset and the green light appeared soon after sunset. He could only guess that what he had seen was one of the many unexplained things associated with nature and God. At some appropriate time, probably in the pub, he could expound his knowledge and assure the good folk that it does not herald a disaster. Then he remembered the Plagues sent to Egypt when the Pharaoh refused Moses' demands, and it left a doubt in his mind.

Thurber was in the store when Ambrose came in for supplies. The two men struck up a conversation and the Rector invited the 'Romany' back for coffee; he too had realised that Ambrose was no normal person. Thurber bustled around the kitchen in making the coffee and even found some biscuits.

"Have you been on the road for a long period?" he asked.

"For quite a number of years," answered Ambrose.

"I suppose most people incorrectly call you a gypsy," Thurber placed the cups on the table, "and they suspect you of all sorts of crime."

Ambrose smiled, "Sometimes it's more than suspect; I've spent a few days in the local cells or been driven on by intolerance and stupidity."

"But you're not a Romany," Thurber offered the sugar bowl, "I have never heard a Romany or a gypsy with that accent!"

"That is a long story!" Ambrose said, "Perhaps one day I will tell it to you."

"Are you staying long in the village?"

"For as long as I am accepted," Ambrose sipped his coffee, "So far the villagers have been at least polite."

"They are just normal people and not involved in deep subjects and convoluted thinking." Thurber produced a flask of whisky and offered a drop in the coffee that Ambrose accepted.

"It was just simple normal people who placed me in the cells and drove me away."

Thurber held up a finger, "You would probably find that it was just one or two ignorant people who stirred up the populace; they are easily led astray."

"I can accept that!"

Thurber changed the subject, "Did you see that green sky the other night?"

Ambrose shook his head, "I have heard about it from some of the people, but I never witnessed it."

"It was most peculiar; in all my years I have never seen such a thing!" Thurber shook his head, "It reminded me of the Ten Plagues of Egypt in the Bible, but when I researched it, I found out that such things are very common."

"I have heard that the Plagues were the result of natural causes and not the punishment of a God."

"You're not a believer then?" Thurber asked.

"I have found that there are more questions in the Bible and the Quran than can be reasonably answered," Ambrose smiled an apology.

"I agree with you," Thurber tapped the table with his forefinger, "but it is all a matter of faith."

"Another word could be trust," the 'Romany' replied, "I have not seen very much of that in my travels."

"Is that what you are looking for?"

CHAPTER FIVE

JOSH AND A VAMPIRE

It was enough to make the milk curdle! Martin Benyan had just collected the villager's milk from the dairy farm, when Old Moses, usually unperturbed by almost anything, was startled by a dim figure in the dark morning mist.

Martin peered at the shape but it kept changing as the streamers of mist drifted across the dark morning landscape. It had rained during the night and the warm air had created the mist, almost a fog in places and made vision difficult.

The figure had vanished and Martin thought that it might have been a cow that had escaped from its field; it was certainly big enough! Old Moses moved on with a little coaxing and Martin looked along the rough road surface; whatever was there would have left tracks, but there was no sign of hooves, paws, or feet!

Perhaps it was a mixture of his mind playing tricks with the drifting mist. He dismissed it and by the time he arrived at the first delivery, Mr and Mrs Maddox, he had forgotten the incident completely.

Miss Julia Probert rang the police in Felixstowe to report an intruder but it was some time before the police car arrived and they found nothing of interest, apart from her vegetable garden was a mess. They concluded that probably a deer or two had helped themselves to a breakfast. Miss Probert looked at her vegetable patch after the police had left, and she saw no signs of small hoof prints that would have been made by the deer.

The real sensation for the day was from Josh Randal, a dubious character that lived just outside the village in a rundown cottage. He came running, a strange experience for him, into the village and banged on the door of the store. George opened the door in his nightgown to see Josh completely out of breath and his face as white as snow.

It took a while and two cups of tea for Josh to explain his appearance. According to him, he was on an early morning walk through the forest when he saw an enormous beast.

"It was Dracula, honest to God it was!" The tea was replaced by a glass of whisky.

"What were you doing in the woods at that hour?" George asked.

Josh looked shifty, "I often take a walk in the woods early in the day." It was a well-known fact that Josh was an accomplished poacher.

George let the answer slide, "Can you describe this monster?"

"It was just like in the films," Josh said excitedly, "big wings and terrible eyes."

"Did you see the fangs?" Mrs Sommers asked.

Josh shook his head and started trembling, so George poured a whiskey and another for himself.

Mrs Sommers continued to ask questions, "Did it fly away?"

Josh had stopped answering and sat there drinking the whisky without tea.

George rang Roland Thurber, "It's Josh Randal, he was up to his tricks in the woods this morning and saw something that has really scared him! He is sitting in my lounge and drinking all of my whisky and he really needs some comforting. Can you come over?"

Thurber arrived within minutes and listened mainly to Mrs Sommers, "It was a big dark thing with wings, and Josh says that it was a vampire, like that Dracula in the films."

The priest turned to Josh, "You do know that the story of Dracula is fiction, don't you? It was written by Bram Stoker over a hundred years ago."

Josh just stared at Thurber with blood-shot eyes.

"I think that we should call the doctor," Thurber suggested, "Josh needs some professional help!"

Doctor David Trower arrived in a bad mood; he had spent all night delivering a baby and just got to sleep when the telephone rang. He examined Josh quickly and decided to take him to the Felixstowe hospital directly.

"Absolute tosh! All of this nonsense about vampires is the product of idle minds!" he snapped as he closed is bag, "I wouldn't be surprised to find that he is a substance abuser. Now help me get him in the car."

CHAPTER SIX

NOSEY THURBER

It was not accidental that Thurber wandered into Ambrose's campsite later that day. The 'Romany' was down by the river filling a large water can, which he stopped doing when he saw the priest.

"I've just come to be nosey," Thurber said with a wide smile.

"Oh you're welcome to be sure; at least you made an honest excuse," Ambrose's country accent had reappeared, "Would you like some tea or coffee, or perhaps something stronger; I understand that the clergy like a tot now and then."

"That is true," Thurber nodded, "but only in moderation; I'll take some plain coffee, thank you."

"Do you often make caravan visits?" Ambrose produced two cups from the caravan.

Thurber laughed, "This is the first! When I was a boy, there were quite a few we used to see in the summer but today they are quite rare."

"It's a more gentle way to travel," Ambrose agreed.

"Have you heard anything about one of the villagers having a big scare last night?"

Ambrose shook his head, "I have not seen anyone else today. What was the problem?"

"He saw a vampire!"

Ambrose looked sharply at the priest, "Is he mentally deranged? Vampires are supposed to come in all shapes and sizes; what sort was this?" The country accent had disappeared.

"Like those horror films by Hammer Studios," Thurber spread his arms, "Big black wings and such."

"Poor fellow!" Ambrose returned to making the coffee, "Christopher Lee could be quite frightening but I always thought that it was too theatrical, too camp! Where was this?"

"On the other side of the village where the woods begin," Thurber waved a vague hand, "The fellow has the reputation for being a poacher, so I suppose he was doing that at the time."

"Well, I've been known to take a rabbit or two in the past, but I know that the woods at night can be scary." Ambrose passed a cup to the priest, "I have had a scare or two with the shapes some things can take on; perhaps the wind of some animal causes something like a bush to move and look threatening."

"Josh has been doing this thing for years, and he has never looked like this before," Thurber sipped the coffee, "The doctor has sent him off to Felixstowe Hospital."

"Does he have some bad habits, this Josh?" Ambrose lit his pipe and the blue smoke curled around their words, somehow joining them.

"Probably!" Thurber answered, "I have heard that there are some magic mushrooms in the area, and if anyone would know where they are, it would be Josh."

"Psilocybin mushroom! I haven't seen any for years," Ambrose smiled, "That was many years ago in my youth with a young lady." His knowledge of the plant's name revealed a better education than most Romanys.

"I am concerned that his story may have an element of truth," Thurber admitted.

"You don't believe in vampires and werewolves, do you?" Ambrose's smiled grew wider.

"As I said to you earlier, it is a matter of believing, having faith where nothing else exists."

"I don't believe in much," Ambrose said, "and I do not believe in ghosts and such; they are just figments of someone's creative mind."

"That is what I thought for many years," Thurber admitted, "Now I am having second thoughts."

CHAPTER SEVEN

FELIXSTOWE HOSPITAL

Doctor Trower was also having second thoughts; after a week, he called in at the Felixstowe Hospital to see how Josh was progressing. The psychiatrist, Pamela Roche, was puzzled at what she had or had not discovered.

"I cannot discover what has caused his delusion; he really thinks that there was a vampire in the woods!" she said, "Has he always acted in strange ways, saw things that were not there?"

"Far from it!" Trower replied, "If anything, mentally he is as hard as nails without any delusions. He would be the last person to suffer a breakdown! What puzzles me is that he has not a TV and as far as I can tell, he has never been to the cinema and he cannot read, so where did he hear about vampires?"

"He doesn't want to go home," said Roche, "He lives alone doesn't he? What is it like, his home?"

Trower laughed, "The first word that comes to mind is disgusting; it has never been cleaned! He is from another era when many people lived off the land, and sometimes illegally. There are always dead animals laying around, rabbits, pheasants, and sometimes a deer. It smells awful and I cannot see anyone else wanting to live like that and his cottage is off the beaten track so he gets little if any visitors."

"He does not appear to want company," said Roche who then turned up her nose, "We had to shower him twice and change his clothes."

"He occasionally goes to the pub, just a couple of times a year," Trower tried to recall details, "The only time I see him is when he has really hurt himself, other than that he appears self-sufficient."

"That's what I get from talking to him," Roche frowned, "but he is really scared to even step outside of these doors; totally out of character, wouldn't you say?" Trower nodded. "The good thing is that he doesn't need close supervision or locking in; he is so scared!" Roche stood up, "Do you want to see him?"

Josh looked surprised to see Trower, "Hello Doc! What do you want? Have you found that thing?"

"'Fraid not, if it had wings it has probably flown away," Trower tried to calm the poacher.

"Just watch it!" Josh looked hastily out of the window, "There is something very nasty out there; just watch out!"

Trower spent about half an hour talking to Josh, but every time that the conversation veered towards that night, Josh started to show some agitation. The fact that hard-headed Josh was so affected by the experience that the doctor started to wonder about alternative explanations.

It was Georgie and Sam, the reluctant schoolchildren who found the next odd thing during one of their usual illicit escapades along the river. There were imprints in the mud of a large bird, at least that was what they first thought.

"It must be larger than an eagle," Georgie said, "it's bigger than my foot, almost twelve inches!"

"What's bigger than an eagle?" Sam wondered.

"A condor, but they are in South America," Georgie replied, "I saw that on TV the other night but this looks bigger than that!"

Nervously they looked about, but seeing nothing, they continued towards their favourite fishing spot.

Sam stopped in his tracks, "Look at this!" He pointed at the ground and then pointed at the trail leading through the mud and weeds. As clear as daylight, the large prints appeared again and wandering down the path to the water.

"Something odd here mate!" Sam said, "This bird has four legs!" Sure enough, the prints displayed the pattern of a four-legged creature walking along.

"Crocodile?" hazarded Georgie.

"Nah! They leave a mark with the tail."

"Do you think that it's in the water?" Georgie said nervously, thinking what he could hook on his line.

"Dunno mate, but it's as big as a pony!" Sam measured the stretch between the prints by walking along them.

"A pony with claws!" Georgie turned back towards home and Sam quickly joined him.

They arrived in Georgie's home; his parents were both at work. Helping themselves to a slice of cake in the kitchen, Georgie opened a large book on the table.

"Look at that!" he pointed to an illustration; it was of a dragon, complete with wings and a scaly tail. "And there is also this!" Again it was an illustration of something similar but with smaller wings, "That's a griffon, and very dangerous!"

"But that's kid's stuff!" Sam objected.

"But what if they were real!" Georgie replied. Sam quietly reflected on the idea.

"We would have seen or heard about them by now," said Sam, "or even seen them in a zoo!"

"Not if they were rare!" Georgie persisted, "I saw on TV that many creatures are disappearing, becoming extinct they call it, endangered species!"

"Nah!" Sam shook his head, "If it were rare, there would be all those guys with binoculars and cameras swarming around like they do with rare birds."

"Yeah, when they hear of them!" Georgie dropped crumbs onto the book, "but they have not heard of this!"

"Okay, if you're right, who do we tell?" Sam folded his arms, "'Cos I'm not going near one of those!" and he thumped the book.

CHAPTER NINE

THURBER BECOMES WORRIED

June arrived in an unexpected burst of sun and heat; the cricket players assembled at the Wooley Shepherds Arms on the first Sunday in their blazing whites and tossed a shiny coin to decide who should bat first.

Martin Benyan, having delivered the Sunday milk on the previous day was on the batting team, and quietly sipping a lemonade while he watched the play. The still air carried the sound of leather on willow – crack, and then the scamper of boots making another run, followed by gentlemanly applause.

"I don't know why I attempt to start services in the summer!" Thurber came up behind Benyan and took the deckchair next to him. His grumble was good natured and produced a smile on the milkman's face.

"You could think that cricket is a religious ceremony; it is always on a Sunday!" Benyan replied.

"I know that to some people it is a religion!" Thurber answered, "Perhaps I should start the service on the village green as part of the competition since the congregation is here."

"Doc Trower is on form!" Benyan pointed as the batsmen scored another run.

"He has an interesting case at the moment."

The milkman nodded, "So I hear; something about old Josh having nightmares. Didn't think he was the type!"

"You wander around at odd hours, at dawn or earlier," Thurber said, "have you seen anything strange and inexplicable?"

Benyan shook his head, and then stopped suddenly, "I had almost forgotten! A little while ago on a misty morning, Moses was reluctant to carry on; something on the road made him nervous and he is usually unconcerned by most things. In the mist, I thought that it might be a cow, it was certainly big, and then it disappeared and we continued. If Moses had not reacted as he did, I would not have remembered!"

"When was this?"

"Um, about the time of the green flash, just after I think!" Benyan stood up, "My turn to bat, wish me luck!"

"Break a leg!" Thurber replied with a smile, but he watched Benyan thoughtfully as the milkman walked to the wicket. He had a feeling for some time that something was happening, like when there is static electricity in the air that makes your hair on your arms stand on end.

After a while, he went back to the church and sat quietly with his thoughts; he could still hear the crack of the bat and the gentle applause. He had the records going back at least one thousand years, and although they were difficult to read in Latin and Old English, he had translations made that were easier to handle than the fragile velum. Every now and then, there were periods of local unrest, of strange comings and goings, the appearances of beings, this had been taken as superstitious nonsense in the past, but now Thurber wondered.

Bishopmount was an odd place, probably the oddest in England; the Vikings had landed nearby but had vanished without explanation, and the Romans avoided the area stating that the area was too wet, too boggy but they had built fortifications up the coast on similar ground. One recent find indicated that something had scared the Roman troops without stating what it was. An old superstition states that you should never mention the name of something evil; perhaps that was it. Something evil not to be spoken.

Evil has many names other than Satan, depending on who is speaking, Christian, Jew, Moslem, or Hindu, and what of those ancient races and their beliefs. Two thousand years ago, even the name of the Emperor Nero was considered evil, a manifestation of everything mad and bad!

What had the milkman seen on the road on that misty morning? What was that green light in the sky? Why had Ambrose appeared at just that time, and what was he? Finally, what was it that scared Josh out of his wits, something that the Romans had seen?

Thurber lit a candle and prayed for a long while for guidance.

CHAPTER TEN

JOSH AND WRAITHS

There was a terrible cry that filled the air and the minds of all who heard it, coming from the psychiatric ward at Felixstowe Hospital, bringing nurses and doctors running. Pamela Roche heard it from the carpark as she was arriving, and despite the distance, she was one of the first to arrive.

Josh had pulled the mattress on to the floor and was cowering under the bed, clutching the mattress and blanket over his head. Roche went on to her hands and knees, trying to coax Josh out but all she could see was his frightened eyes from behind the blanket; there was also a strong smell of vomit.

After a while, they extracted him whimpering and sat him in a chair so that he could be examined. He was covered in vomit and excrement, so whatever had happened had given him a big fright. A strong injection calmed him down, almost unconscious, and the nurses cleaned up the mess and remade the bed; all that was needed now was to get Josh cleaned up. With the help of a male nurse, he was almost carried into the bathroom, his clothing removed and a warm shower appeared to comfort him and bring him partially to his senses.

"Josh, Josh," Now that he was clean and dressed, Roche called his name until he looked at her, "What happened Josh? What upset you?"

Immediately his eyes started search the room, "It was here, looking at me with those eyes!"

"What was here?" Roche asked.

"That thing, that vampire!" Josh was becoming excited again.

"The one that you saw in the forest?"

Josh nodded rapidly. Roche looked at the male nurse, "Has anyone been here in the last hour or two?"

"I don't think so, but I can check. Will you be alright alone with him?" When she nodded, he left them. He quickly came back with a shake of his head, "No one, and it's well before visitors." When they tried to take him back to his room, Josh backed away.

"There's no one here Josh, look!" Roche stepped through the doorway and spun around, "See? It's just me and nothing else!"

Hesitatingly, Josh stepped into the room and looked nervously in all of the corners. Roche sat him in a chair and sat on the bed holding his hand. The male nurse stayed by the door as a precaution.

"Josh, where did you learn about vampires?" she asked.

"I found a comic about vampires and other things, bad things!" His hands began to shake, "They are real, and I saw one!"

"They are not real Josh," Roche took both hands to comfort him, "Some people like those stories and some people like to dress up like them, especially at Halloween; they are not real and perhaps you saw one of those in a costume."

Josh shook his head violently, "I know about Halloween, I've seen the dead in the churchyard rise up! That thing, that vampire was here in my room, it wants me!"

Roche was startled about the mention of the churchyard; this was something new! She began to change her ideas about what was wrong with Josh, but first she had to check out a few things.

"Josh, can I leave you in the hands of Harry here," Roche pointed to the make nurse, "he will stay with you until I return. Is that OK?"

Josh looked at Harry and nodded, help by the big smile Harry gave.

"Don't leave him for a second, "she instructed, "I just have to check a few things."

She overshot the turning for Bishopmount as the sign was quite obscured. A mile further on, she discovered her mistake and turned back, driving slower so as not to miss the turning. As she drove down the narrow lane with green hedgerows, she had the impression that she was entering a different world, perhaps a different time.

The church was obvious to find, and she parked outside in the shade of a Yew tree, looking at the lynch gate and the churchyard beyond.

"It's the Death Tree you know!" The voice came behind her and made her jump. On turning, she saw that it was a priest, "Roland Thurber! Sorry to startle you but the Yew tree has that reputation."

"Oh, it's alright and I was just using the shade," she smiled, "Doctor Pamela Roche from the hospital at Felixstowe."

"Ah, that is where they took Josh!" Thurber nodded, "Is it him that you want to know about?"

"Yes and no!" Roche looked flustered, "He said something today that is decidedly weird, he said that he has seen the dead rise from their graves. Earlier I had the impression that he didn't believe in such things, so I came to nose around and correct some preconceived ideas."

Thurber chuckled, "Wraiths!"

"Pardon!"

"Wraiths, I've seen them for myself," Thurber admitted, "There is something odd about the ground around here and every so often, there are streams of mist emanating for the graves and other places. I have a theory that was why the Romans didn't like the place two thousand years ago and left."

"I see! It's some geological phenomenon!" Roche laughed, "I wondered what sort of place this was, especially when you said that you had seen them."

"Come in, come in!" Thurber led her through the gate, "Any old place is bound to have some imaginary monsters, but I am worried about Josh. He's not really a parishioner, although he lives on the edge of the village in a horrible old cottage. All alone since his father died years ago, that's his grave there, but he never comes here."

"How old is the village?" Roche asked.

"Heaven knows! The church is 9th century, but there was something heathen on the site before that, possibly Neolithic as the village, under various names, as been here as long as there have been people in England."

"So lots of history!" Roche looked interested, "and that means lots of stories!"

Thurber chuckled again, "Most of them originating in the Wooley Shepherds Arms over there," he pointed across the green, "It's harmless enough stories but now and then things do get out of hand."

"In what way?"

"Strange pranks played by some joker," Thurber pulled his bottom lip, "things go missing and then turn up somewhere else, or someone starts a rumour that runs amok. No great harm really."

"Would someone have played a prank on Josh?"

"I wouldn't think so," Thurber shook his head, "People play pranks on people they know, and Josh was a solitary soul!"

"So no one dressed up as Dracula to scare him witless?" Roche looked for confirmation, but Thurber had turned away and was walking towards the rectory.

"Can I offer you some refreshment?" he asked, "I have some very pleasant Earl Grey tea that you would like."

"Thank you, and while we do that, you can tell me about the village and its residents."

Thurber chuckled, "Then you'll stay for a while! There are more stories than there have been residents!"

"I don't mind staying in a rural setting for a few days, maybe even a bit longer if the company is of good quality!"

CHAPTER ELEVEN

OLD MOSES WANDERS

Most publicans are the last people to retire for the night; having served everyone and sent the last customers home to their wives or lovers; there is the matter of tidying everything, actual cleaning can wait until the morning cockerel, he continued counting the till and locking up everything securely before succumbing to the world of dreams.

Trevor Watts had just locked away the day's takings and was turning out the lights; the last ones illuminated the front door and the sign of a grinning shepherd holding a large ram. As he reached for the switch, he saw a shadowy figure on the village green, just beyond the power of the lights. Trevor shook his head, the fumes of alcohol must have irritated his eyes because he could not make out the shape, it flittered and moved like a sheet in the wind, a dark sheet at that!

Uncertain of what to do, he shrugged his shoulders and switched off the light and as he shut the door, the chimes of midnight rang aloud from the church. For some reason, a shiver ran down his spine and he ran to his bed.

"What's wrong with you?" his wife asked.

Trevor shook his head, "It's nothing, I'm probably getting a cold!"

"You never catch colds," Mrs Watts said, "You told me that with all of the alcohol and cigarette fumes no germ dares to venture!"

Trevor grunted a reply and buried his head under the blankets. Well before the sun's first rays lit the sky, he rose and went to the window; the vision that he had of whatever was on the green had continued to haunt his sleep. Although he had put it down to a loose sheet or tarpaulin, he was sure now that it was some creature, so donning his overcoat and shoes he went and opened the door, collecting a flashlight on the way.

As he stepped onto the village green, the flashlight revealed a familiar shape of Old Moses, the milk float horse quietly chewing grass. Somehow, he had escaped from his paddock and Benyan will be looking for him soon. With a small laugh and a sigh, Trevor picked up the bridle and headed towards the paddock; it was not far but Trevor would lose some precious sleep.

As they walked down the lane, Trevor began to think; what he saw was nothing like the shape of a horse. Nervously, he looked over his shoulder and for a moment he could have sworn that there was something fluttering at the edge of vision, or perhaps not.

Benyan was surprised and pleased by the return of Old Moses, "He has never left the paddock before, even if the gate was open."

Trevor felt nervous about returning alone down the dark country lane to the village, so he took a coffee with the milkman while chatting and inviting himself on the milk cart to take him home. When they arrived at the Wooley Shepherds Arms, he thanked Benyan and then stood looking thoughtfully over the village green, as the sun rose in a misty dawn and that is where his wife found him.

"What are you doing?" she asked.

"Hmm! I was just thinking if that pond was ever used as a ducking pool," he continued to stand and look.

"What an earth for?" Mrs Watts looked at him in mock humour, "Are you thinking of ducking me?"

Trevor shook his head and gave a quite laugh, "I was thinking about all of the witch stories in this area; by all accounts, there was a lot going on."

"And pigs can fly!"

"Watch out, there is a squadron of pigs assembling!" Finally, Trevor turned to catch up on his sleep.

CHAPTER TWELVE

NEWSPAPER HOUND

Jean Ryder had an intriguing mystery; she had a cousin who lived in Bishopmount who had come to her with a story of a mysterious green light, a lone gypsy, and strange creatures seen abroad. As a budding journalist, this smelled of a story and so she arrived in search of facts in her Volkswagen.

Her cousin Ralph Ryder was a lot older and earned a living as a carpenter. Usually, it was replacing fences or restoring a chair; occasionally he would be asked to undertake a bigger task and a lot of the church interior was his handiwork, as well as some of the old cottages.

He was one of the publican's 'guests' that saw the green light that evening, and as he worked all over the area, he began to collect stories and it was these that he had sent on to Jean. Some of the stories were obvious fabrications, imitations of an original story, repeated from other sources, but some had a sense of fantastic reality.

Ralph was working on a carving in his workshop when Jean arrived; he looked up and squinted through the motes of wood-dust at the silhouette framed in the doorway.

"Hello Ralph, it's me, Jean!"

Ralph blinked for a moment, and then his brain connected with the words, "Come in girl, sit on that bench while I finish this, and then we can go into the house for a cup of tea."

"I came about the green light and the other stories," she explained, "Were you just tugging at my pigtails, or are they of interest?"

Ralph blew some chippings away, "You can meet the people involved and get the story first hand if you like, and then make up your own mind."

"I looked up about the green light," Jean continued, "it would appear that the Earth's magnetic field is the cause of many types of phenomena, and green light is prominent in most cases."

"I don't know much about magnetic fields," Ralph straightened his back with a grunt, "All I do know is that a whole bunch of funny things have been happening since!"

"Such as?"

"Gardens being trashed…"

"That sounds like some teenage vandals," Jean pointed out.

"We don't have any of those in the area," Ralph countered, "There have been unidentified creatures roaming around, and someone removed the milkman's horse from the paddock."

"Doesn't sound much to me!" Jean said.

"Then there is our local poacher in Felixstowe Hospital scared out of his mind," Ralph replaced the chisel in its rack, "He swears that Count Dracula is in the village!"

"That's better! He must have seen something that reminded him of Dracula, and that makes sense," Janet began to sound enthusiastic.

"Josh Randall is the most unimaginative person you will ever meet," Ralph took off his apron and hung it on a nail, "his cottage is a disgusting slaughterhouse and from what I hear, he had never heard of Dracula until recently."

"What do you think he saw?"

Ralph shrugged his shoulders, "I have no idea and I am not sure that I want to know!"

Jean stood up, "You can treat me to that cup of tea, and I hope that you can put me up for a few days and introduce me to these 'witnesses'."

"Most will be in the Wooley Shepherds Arms tonight, and they will just love telling you their stories over a pint or three. You'll have to make up the bed as no one has used it in a long time."

CHAPTER THIRTEEN

BEER TALES

Thurber sat slightly outside the garrulous group of story tellers that night, slightly amused at their antics towards the pretty girl as their stories became more ridiculous by the pint, and slightly concerned that no one was taking the matter seriously, after all, a man was seriously ill in hospital.

"I tell you that I saw the claw marks on the tree," Giles Nuttock insisted.

James Trumbin shook his head, "What you saw was the damage Old Pepper did when he tried to take his wagon through too smaller gap; I was there and saw him do it!"

"That was another tree!" Taffy Jones joined in the argument, "I saw the marks with Giles."

"But did you see the vampire make the marks?" Jean asked.

"Of course not!" Giles said, "Or we wouldn't be here drinking your ale."

"The young lady has a point," Trumbin interjected, "You have all see the 'evidence' but not the cause. I could go out now and create much more 'evidence' that would propagate even wilder stories."

"What about Josh?" Taffy reminded them, "I wouldn't think that the Devil from Hell would have scared him!"

"What about him," Jean had a small recorder going in her bag, "You're saying that a man with no imagination gets scared of his own shadow."

"Something's shadow Miss, something nasty!" Giles said.

"Something that has been here a very long time," Trumbin said quietly.

"I suppose that I will have to see the scene of the crime for myself," Jean sighed.

"Just don't go at night Miss!"

"I think that I can second that!" Trumbin ordered some more ale.

CHAPTER FOURTEEN

AMBROSE'S PET

Small boys, and even old men, frequently lose track of time. Taking pleasure has an infinite time-line, and boys and men always find some way to have pleasure; simple things like fishing, or sailing boats and complex adventures of the mind; fantasy comes easily to them.

This is what happened with Georgie and Sam when they went on one of their fishing trips. They started later than usual and avoided the spot where they found the 'dragon's claws', and set up their rods, two each, and then settled down with a bottle of lemonade and a pack of sandwiches, their school lunch.

The fish were not biting and they started to play games, such as 'I Spy With My Little Eye', and that made the time fly by faster than ever. They stopped their play when Sam's rod bent and then twanged; they had never heard a rod twang before. It was then that they realised that the day had almost disappeared, but this must be a big fish and they opted to land it before going home.

The line was quivering; the float had sunk out of sight, pulled under the dark waters by the prize-winning fish on the other end of the line, not that they could admit to fishing on a school day. Sam had grabbed the rod with both hands and pulled as hard as he could, and before their surprised eyes, the rod almost bent double. Georgie rushed to help his friend as Sam's feet were sliding on the mud towards the water.

"This must be the biggest catch ever!" Sam gasped with the effort.

Far out from the bank, the water was swirling as though a whirlpool was forming and then the back of something broke the surface to disappear again.

"Did you see the size of that?" Georgie yelled.

"Just a bit!" Sam dug his heels into the mud, "Grab hold of my belt and pull."

Georgie did as asked, but after a few minutes, they fell flat on their backs. Sam wound in the line to find that the hook, bait, and float were missing.

"What fish do you know of that swallows hook, line and sinker?" Sam looked at the line closely.

"We'll have to come back and try again," said Georgie, "it must be a monster?"

"Did you see how the line was behaving?" Sam asked, "It wasn't moving, just vibrating like a violin string."

"I'll take your word for it, but I've never looked closely at a violin." Georgie said as he started to pack up their fishing gear.

They hid the gear in a hollow tree as usual, and carried on homeward through the gathering gloom. Sam suddenly stopped and peered at the track, and then he pointed.

"Can you see that print in the dust, it's not very clear?"

Georgie looked at where Sam was pointing, "Yeah, I can see it; it's our old friend with the big claws!"

Nervously, they looked around; something big with claws was not something that they wanted to meet, especially as night was fast approaching. Despite their apprehension, they started to follow the tracks as they were going in their direction.

Ahead they could hear a man's voice, not loud, even comforting. The boys crept closer until they could see the source of the voice; it was Ambrose standing by his caravan, and he was talking to the clawed monster!

As they had figured out, it had four legs, but what horrified them were the huge wings like a bat and what was certainly a dragon's head. Ambrose was feeding it with some large roots, and as the monster ate, it displayed large fangs,

The boys must have made a noise, or maybe the dragon smelled them. It jerked its head around to look directly at them; Ambrose paused his feeding and walked towards the boys; he was followed by the dragon, but neither of them looked angry.

"I should have guessed!" Ambrose said as the boys came into view.

"We - we wondered what had made those tracks," Sam stuttered.

"Well, now you know!" Ambrose turned towards the dragon, "This is Fandorn, and she is related to the dragons of old."

"Is she going to eat us?" Georgie asked nervously.

There was a surprising gurgle from Fandorn, "I don't eat humans, you're too small!"

"This is why we keep moving," Ambrose explained, "You saw her earlier as the horse that draws the caravan, but she frequently has to return to her normal self, and eventually, we are found out."

"It – she can talk," said Georgie.

"And she swims in our lake," said Sam.

"YOUR lake!" huffed Fandorn, "No one really owns the waters and the mountain; they are a gift for everyone."

"A gift from who?" asked Sam.

"What you call Mother Nature," answered Fandorn.

"What was it that I almost caught in the lake today?" asked Sam.

"That was me!" Fandorn said, "Your hook became caught in one of my scales, so I teased you; nasty things hooks!"

"What will you do now?" Georgie asked.

"That depends on the villagers," Ambrose said, "If you tell them, they will come to see for themselves, but all they will find is a Romany caravan and its horse. They may just shrug it away, or they could make things difficult for us."

"We won't say anything!" Sam said.

"Can you fly?" Georgie asked Fandorn.

Fandorn rustled his leathery wings, "These are not just decoration, but I only fly at night."

"Could you carry someone, someone like me?" continued Georgie.

"Come here tonight and I will give an experience like no other!" Fandorn said.

"She is my best friend and she only hurts people who attack us," said Ambrose, "so we have to do things out of sight of people."

CHAPTER FIFTEEN

JAMIE FINDS A FRIEND

Christine Hannan was the next to discover the remarkable truth about the 'Romany' and his 'horse'. She had been involved in a project that she did not realise the passage of time and it was her dog Jamie who brought her into the present time.

She had hardly said," C'mon boy," when Jamie shot out of the door and was heading for the woods, leaving Christine puffing behind. She had an idea where he was going and when she arrived at the Romany camp she stopped dead in her tracks; there was Jamie looking up at Fandorn and wagging his tail.

She was frozen to the spot! The huge monster trailed its gossamer leather wings on each side of its scaly body and its ferocious dragon's head was bending down towards the dog, but that was all; the four clawed feet were relaxed as Fandorn lay down.

"Jamie is perfectly safe," Ambrose's voice was behind her and made her jump, "My pet will not harm your pet."

"Pet!" Christine croaked as her vocal were paralyzed.

"We have travelled to many places and in all of that time she has never hurt a single creature, except the fish that she so loves to eat. Come and meet Fandorn, she and your Jamie are good friends." Ambrose took her hand and led her forward in a hypnotised state.

`"You are Jamie's friend," Fandorn turned his gaze on to her, "He has been telling me stories about how good it is to live with you; if I was smaller, I would love such a life and he thanks you."

Christine's mouth fell open; she was saturated with strange emotions, surely, this is a dream or a nightmare! Real live dragons that could speak!

"Now, if Ambrose would make some of his wonderful tea, we can spend some time knowing each other," Fandorn said.

The warm mug was pushed into her hand and she sat on a chair that Ambrose fetched while he sat on a log; they sat around the fire as the night descended, Fandorn and Ambrose telling her the story of dragons.

CHAPTER SIXTEEN

FANDORN

Roland Thurber was a keen observer of people; it came with the job. He knew about the boy's illicit fishing by watching their movements, especially when they were seen elsewhere than at school. He had noticed the change in their behaviour, and then Christine came to see him.

At first, she had difficulty in coming to the point; she hummed and hard and left sentences hardly started. Thurber waited with his usual patience, knowing that eventually whatever it was would emerge.

At last, she blurted out, "I have seen a dragon!"

Thurber raised one eyebrow, "What sort of dragon and where was it?" He fully expected to hear that it was a dream.

"It was big and it spoke," Christine's hands were shaking, "While it was speaking, I was not afraid but that was a couple of days ago and now I am wondering if I am going mad; did I talk to a dragon?"

"A talking dragon, that is something I wasn't expecting," Thurber said, "Why is it that no one else has had this conversation?" As he spoke, a thought occurred to him, "Why, the little devils!"

Christine looked questioningly at the priest, "What little devils?"

"Where did you see this dragon?"

"Oh, in Ambrose's camp in the forest, not far from the river," Christine pointed vaguely towards the forest, "And its name is Fandorn."

"The dragon is called Fandorn?" Thurber confirmed the name.

Christine nodded, "Who are the little devils?"

"Georgie and Sam, two clever little fishermen," Thurber shook his head, "Who would believe it? What did this Fandorn tell you?"

"It was the history of the dragons, and we have the wrong idea about them," Christine answered, "they are not all as destructive as in the stories."

"I was in Ambrose's camp a little while ago and I didn't notice a large dragon," Thurber stood up, "I will have a chat with Ambrose and this Fandorn, if I can. Before that I will talk to Georgie and Sam."

CHAPTER SEVENTEEN

THURBER MEETS FANDORN

"We promised not to tell!" Sam said to Thurber. He had found the boys making up some new fishing lines behind the store.

"She took us flying," added Georgie.

"It's a she is it, and she flies?" Thurber said.

"She is very nice, nicer than some people," Sam added.

"That we shall see, but in the meantime, say nothing to anyone," Thurber instructed, "and if it were a school day, I would march you to your lessons."

Thurber waited until midday, and then just wandered into the wood. When he arrived at the camp of Ambrose, only the horse was there.

"I suppose that I can just wait a while," and he sat on the log.

"That depends on who you want to see," the voice came from behind him, and when he turned, all he could see was the horse looking at him.

Thurber looked around and then addressed the horse, "Would I be speaking to the dragon called Fandorn?"

"Who have you been talking to?" Ambrose appeared from another direction.

"Two small boys and a young woman," Thurber sat on the log again, "I can think that you are a ventriloquist and that your tea is some sort of hallucinogen, am I right?"

"And you would be wrong!" the first voice said, and again it appeared to come from the horse.

"That is clever," Thurber addressed the 'Romany'.

"I came across Fandorn a long time ago," Ambrose produced two mugs of tea, "she was in a bad state, got caught in the turbulence in the upper air, and before she knew it, she was on the ground."

"I have much to thank Ambrose for," and when Thurber looked at the horse again, it was now a large winged dragon.

Thurber was shocked; he was certain that this 'dragon thing' was some trick, but seeing the creature before him, its dark green wings outstretched, he realised that it must be true.

"We have to hide as folk are so stupid that they would kill her, or worse, capture her and put her in a zoo. It is fortunate that she has the power to change shape, and so she becomes my 'Romany horse'" Ambrose offered a shot of whiskey for the tea. Thurber decided that he needed it!

Fandorn laid her large head next to the priest, "Because of your technology, I can only fly at night so I fish during the day. The radar can see me, but they put it down to 'ghost' images." The dragon laughed, "If only they knew the truth!"

"Are there any other dragons?" Thurber managed to ask, his nerves now under control.

"Dragon is a recent name," Fandorn said, "In the past I was known here as a Nicor, a water monster, I do love the fish, and the Vikings called me a Wyrm or an Orm, a snake! Do I look like a snake?"

"That is why we are wandering around," Ambrose said, "We are looking for the others, but because of people's prejudices and fears, the other dragons hide, making our task difficult."

"I can imagine so," Thurber nodded, "very wise of them. How many have you found?"

"Seventeen," said Fandorn angrily, "and most of them were in a sorry state; none had a benefactor like Ambrose. We fixed them up but they are in urgent need of protection."

"I can see that," Thurber nodded, "How old are you?"

"I was old when Gilgamesh built the first cities, and even older as I watched the wooden horse enter Ilium, Troy as you call it, to destroy the city, and older still when Christ was crucified. You are a cruel people!"

"I cannot argue with that," Thurber sighed, "My purpose is to eliminate that trait in humans, but we are not doing very well so far."

"What will the villagers do now?" Ambrose asked.

Thurber shrugged, a thought occurred to him that Ambrose may be as old as his pet, "The villagers may not be your biggest problem; if the news of your existence goes into the wider world, and I have no idea what will happen. Perhaps it would be better if you stayed as a horse."

"It is a strange captivity!" said Fandorn forlornly, "the bars are made out of prejudice!"

CHAPTER EIGHTEEN

GREEN LIGHT TWO

For a September night, it was very hot. Christine had thrown back the duvet and still felt uncomfortable, and Jamie was panting to cool down. She got up, went into the kitchen, and poured a glass of cold water, and as she drank, the world turned green.

With the glass still held to her mouth, she turned towards the window; everything was green, the sky glowed as though it was midday, but green. She had missed the first appearance of the green light, and now she saw it first-hand.

As she looked, she heard the clop-clop of a horse's hooves; she looked in sadness as the 'Romany' caravan passed, and just for a moment, she thought that the horse had huge leathery wings, she blinked and it became a normal horse. A brown hand appeared from the caravan and waved, and automatically she waved back. Ambrose and Fandorn had decided to move on before there was a commotion.

As the caravan faded from view, the green sky faded and resumed its normal indigo shade, the stars gleaming and showing the constellation Draco, the Dragon.

THE END

HOUSE GUEST

When Mary and Kenneth Forbes saw the old house, they fell in love with it immediately; it was the large veranda at the front and the large conservatory at the rear that they especially liked. They were expecting their first child, and the house had enough room for any child or more; they envisaged their child playing in the long garden, but before that, the garden needed some loving care.

Mary was trying to establish herself as an artist, and the conservatory would be ideal to relax and let the imagination flow. Kenneth was in IT, so he could work from home and keep an eye on Mary and the child. It was an ideal plan!

Kenneth's brother, Barry and his wife Bernie came round to help with the decorating; Mary had no family, which is why the baby, the house and everything were so important to her. The idea was that the interior should be light, so everything was white, light grey and pastel colours. That was the plan, but as so often happens, it did not work out that way; one room would not take the paint and the walls were streaky and stayed that way until Kenneth found that a strong green colour was acceptable. As this was at the side of the house, it would serve as his study.

They moved in at the end of September; it had been warm all year, but on that day, it rained a flood! Kenneth was eager to clear the garden, but in that weather, it would have to wait. They sat in the conservatory and watched a solid wall of water saturate the trees and bushes. The drumming of the rain on the conservatory roof gave Mary a headache, and she went to lie of the sofa in the living room, and soon fell asleep.

Kenneth opened his laptop and started to work, and he was unaware that the time had passed and night was coming on. It was a clap of thunder that made him aware of the time, and that Mary had not come back from her rest. Puzzled, he walked into the living room to see how she was. For a moment, he was sure that there was someone else in the room and standing near Mary. She was still sound asleep, and Kenneth gently caressed her face; she murmured and turned her head, and then her eyes flew open.

"Oh God!" she said softly, "That was such a lovely dream."

Kenneth smiled, "What was it about?"

"I was talking to Leonard," she said dreamily.

"Leonard who?" he asked.

"Our baby, he is so awfully clever,"

Kenneth was more than surprised as they had not bothered to find out the baby's gender, and here was Mary dreaming it was a boy, "It is late, shall I make a light supper?"

"Hmm, with lots of toast and something fishy; Leonard loves fish," Mary wriggled on her back and snuggled into the pillow.

"I'll see what we have," Kenneth went to the kitchen and looked in the fridge and then in the cupboards; he found a tin of sardines and then he started the toaster. He shook his head as he thought of Mary's dream. He knew that pregnant women could behave in peculiar ways, but he had not heard on one talking to the unborn child.

When he took the supper into the living room, Mary was still asleep; gently he woke her.

"Oh, that looks and smells delightful. Thank you darling!" and she began to eat ravenously.

***

Kenneth was in the garden when Mary's water broke. He flung down the tools, raced into the conservatory and picked her up to place her in the car. He rang Barry and then roared off to the hospital, breaking several speed limits on the way.

He was pacing up and down in the hospital reception when Barry and Bernie arrived, "How is she?" they asked.

Kenneth shrugged, "They took her off a few minutes ago, and said that they would fetch me in a while."

"Do you want to see the birth?" Bernie asked.

"Dunno! Do I or don't I?" Kenneth had never smoked, but he felt like one now.

His dilemma was solved by a nurse calling him into the birth room. Mary was making whoosh noises and grunting. He moved over to her side and she took his hand in a vice-like grip. During a pause, she laid back sweating and smiled at him, "Leonard said it would be today!"

"You are determined that it is a 'he'," Kenneth winced under her grip.

"You wait and see," Mary gasped, "and he will be a genius, just like his old man,"

Kenneth did not feel like a genius, in fact he felt like he was at the bottom of IQ range. With a final scream and a push, a little red bundle of humanity lay on the bed while the nurse cut the umbilical cord. Kenneth peeked, and saw that it was a son with a fine head of hair.

He looked at his wife and nodded, "It's a Leonard!"

She squealed with delight, "Never doubt me again, Mister Forbes!"

***

Leonard started to stand at about six months of age, wobbling unsteadily around the living room, and occasionally sitting down with a thump. After that he started to put sounds together to make a sentence, there was not very much time for baby talk.

Bernie had produced twins in the meantime, and the three children played together most of the time. Leonard had his first birthday, and as it was fair weather, they held a barbeque on the patio of the old house.

"I think that our kids are retarded, compared to Leonard," Bernie said as she watched Leonard romp around, while hers were still crawling.

"He is older," Mary pointed out, "and there are always differences between children. They are okay!"

"I was in the clinic a few days ago, just a checkup," Bernie said, "and the children there were nothing as advanced as Leonard. Hearing his name, the infant came toddling over.

"Bee!" he said firmly and touched Bernie's knee.

"I think that he said your name!" Mary gasped, "My clever lad!" So there was no mistake, Leonard repeated the sound and pointed to Bernie.

"Kenneth, come here, Leonard has just said Bernie's name."

Leonard performed the trick again. "Blast!" Kenneth said, "I hoped that it would be one of ours, or at least Mummy and Daddy."

From that time on, Leonard's vocabulary increased exponentially. Shortly after that, Kenneth was reading a report when he found his son looking over his shoulder, "What are all those squiggles?" the boy asked.

Kenneth explained about the alphabet, and that the squiggles were the same as spoken words. Then the boy said something remarkable, "Do those squiggles mean the same in every language?" Where did the boy learn about the different languages? He thought back to his childhood and concluded that he was at least seven years older than his son was now when he learned that there were other languages than English.

"He doesn't need to speak," Mary said, "He and I talk all of the time; I know exactly what is in his head!"

Kenneth looked at her with a blank expression, "You said that when he was in your womb, and as you were both at that time a single person, it makes sense, I think, but now you're saying he is a telepath!"

"There is always a link between mother and child," Mary answered, "however old the child becomes."

"What do you talk about?"

"Oh, everything," Mary said, "He was asking about reading and writing almost as soon as he was born, and that is why I think that he learned so quickly."

"He doesn't talk to me!" Kenneth complained.

"Well, you weren't pregnant!" Mary smirked.

***

When Leonard started school, the teachers could not believe his age, "He is ahead of every other pupil in this school," the head mistress said, "How are his numbers?"

It turned out that Leonard's mathematical skills were on a par with his language skills, "We should put him in a special school," the headmistress suggested.

"We are not sure that is the right thing to do," said Kenneth and Mary, "we do not want him to feel different from the other kids."

"He is different though," the headmistress pointed to a far table where Leonard was working with some other children, "He is teaching the other children; there is little reason for me to be here!"

The decision was held in abeyance while Mary and Kenneth talked things over.

"I have a feeling that whatever we do will be the wrong decision," Kenneth said.

"I am sure that he needs physical contact with other children," Mary added.

"Yes, I agree, but mentally he is light years ahead of other children," Kenneth said, "and that would do a lot of harm. He needs someone who can talk on his level."

"What is his level?"

They had Leonard's IQ tested but the conclusion was vague, the tester saying that there must be something wrong with the test. She refused to reveal the results, as she did not believe that an infant would give such high readings.

"Does he still talk to you?" Kenneth asked Mary.

Mary nodded, "He wants to be with other bright kids, he can search for them on whatever he uses for a network, but so far nothing that satisfies him."

Kenneth looked at his wife with his jaw off latch, "He can read everyone's mind?"

"Of course! That part of him developed faster than anything else," Mary smiled, "It is pretty terrifying to think of it. He does not want anyone else to know, as some people would do something bad to him and us."

"Politicians for a start," Kenneth grinned, "They tell more lies than anyone else."

"He agrees with you," Mary said.

"Is he reading my mind as well?" Kenneth rubbed his head.

***

"He wants to come here!" Leonard stated at breakfast one day.

"Who wants to come here?" Kenneth asked.

Leonard made a strange noise, "That's the name, and he is very clever.

"Where does he come from?" Mary asked.

Leonard pointed up at the ceiling. Kenneth and Mary looked up at the ceiling.

"Someone in the loft?" Kenneth made a stab at what his son was saying.

Leonard burst out laughing, spreading cereal everywhere, "No silly, he lives in a strange place that he just calls home, and he is on his way here!"

Kenneth leaned back in his chair and continued looking at the ceiling, "The only thing above the house is space! Is he from another planet?"

Leonard nodded, "Of course! There are many minds out there, but not all of them are smart or nice, so I block their connection."

"You can block any connection?" Kenneth asked.

"Yeah, I have put a block around you both so that they will not harm you," Leonard casually continued eating his breakfast.

Kenneth looked at his young son, not yet in long trousers, and wondered what sort of offspring he and Mary had produced. It was because of this remarkable son, that Mary had decided not to have any more children; another like Leonard would be too much.

***

Leonard was sitting on a garden bench, staring at the ground; it was difficult to tell if he was asleep or thinking. As Mary walked towards him, he held up a finger, and then it was obvious that he was probably thinking. He did this very often, and the first few times it threw both parents into a panic with thoughts of autism and epilepsy but it became obvious that he was 'talking' to someone of something.

"He is here!" Leonard announced.

Mary whirled round, and then up on the roof and at the driveway, nothing could be seen.

"Your friend from up there?" Mary asked, pointing skywards.

Leonard nodded with his head still held down, "Yeah, he is here. He realises that you cannot pronounce his name, so you can call him Terrance."

Mary looked wildly around again, "Where is he? Where is Terrance?"

Leonard pointed to his own head, "He's in here!"

"Hello Mary!" From Leonard's lips came a deep voice, "Do not be frightened! My physical form is on a different wavelength than yours, so you cannot see me, nor can I speak and I use Leonard's voice. I am pleased to meet you."

Mary just stood and gaped, and then she stuttered, "You're welcome, I'm sure."

Kenneth saw from his study window that Mary appeared to be having a conversation with Leonard, and then he noticed that his wife was obviously upset. "Anything wrong Dear?" he called out and Mary waved for him to come out.

"Terrance is here!" Mary said as Kenneth walked towards them.

"Hello Kenneth, I am Terrance, the person you have been waiting for," the voice said, "Do not be alarmed."

Kenneth reached out and took his wife under his arm, "You are this person from another planet, another star?"

"Certainly a different place than this one," Terrance said.

"Can I get you a drink or something?" Mary had remembered her manners, "Oh silly me, you probably cannot drink! Sorry!"

"Do not trouble yourselves on my account," Terrance gave a short laugh, "my drinking and eating habits are unlike yours; thank you for the kind thought."

For the rest of the day, they conversed with alternative Leonard and Terrance. When Kenneth asked Terrance about his home planet, the reply was always vague, Terrance saying that he could not convey a description that they would understand.

After supper, Terrance appeared to have retired or retreated, and Leonard was his usual self. He said good night to his parents and went to bed. For a while, Mary and Kenneth were quiet, absorbing the state of affairs. They listened for any noise from the boy's bedroom, but all was still.

"I wonder if Terrance can hear us even when Leonard isn't with us!" He mused.

"I feel like screaming!" Mary said quietly, "There is a creature here that has no right to exist in our world."

"We, the humans may be able to learn a lot from this creature, and God knows what other things he has been talking to!" Kenneth took her hand.

"That thought has also occurred to me," Mary began to tremble, "Can you imagine a house full of aliens that we cannot see or speak directly to them?"

"I am sure that this will be the only one," Kenneth asserted. Eventually, they went to bed and after a few sleepless dozing minutes, they fell asleep.

Mary had a dream, a dream that made her moan and toss around. Finally, she woke up and saw a figure by the bed; it was Leonard, but not the Leonard that she knew.

He was crouching over his father, a father that had no throat and everything was soaked in blood. From her son's mouth, Terrance's voice spoke, "You should sleep Mary, it is only a dream."

As she threw back the sheets and started to scream, a force blocked her voice and pushed her back on the bed, "You and I have spoken together for many years, ever since you saw this house for the first time. I am the Spirit of the House. It was I who taught your boy to talk and read, he and I are the same person!"

Mary lost consciousness, which was just as well.

The Weekly Echo

News Item One: The mutilated bodies of Mary and Kenneth Forbes were found late this morning, and their six year old son Leonard is missing. The police suspect that a wild animal has entered the house and murdered the couple and then carried off the boy.

News Item Two: The mutilated bodies of Bernadette and Barry Forbes were discovered earlier today…

THE END

BROTHER MINE

The earliest part of the winter's day, when the sun struggles to shed light through the mist shrouded trees; everything appears to move slowly, even the birds chirp and fly in slow motion through the frozen air. Most of them preferred to sit in the trees and look at the scene below them.

The soil clunked soggily on the wooden lid.

"You would think that would be it," Davis Charters said.

"You're going to tell me different?" his brother Ferris gave a sigh, "Apart from some fairy tales, I always thought that this the final destination."

Davis looked around, "None of the rest of the family has seen fit to attend." The only figures were the two sextons waiting patiently, and the retiring backs of the priest and pall bearers.

"Do you really think that they would?" Ferris grunted, "You are the blackest sheep in any family! Now shall we move off and let them finish the planting?" He placed the black fedora firmly on his head.

Davis sniggered, "You always have a quaint way of saying things." As they drifted away, the sexton and his assistant continued piling the soil into the grave, thunk, thunk.

"Some people came to watch; friends of yours?" Ferris nodded towards another part of the churchyard. A group of people, including a child or two, stood watching as the grave filled up; the odd thing about them was that they wore inadequate clothing for such a cold winter's day.

Davis shook his head, "Never seen them before, but they seem to know us!" Some of them were waving them over, "Perhaps they will hold a wake!"

"That will not do you a lot of good as you no longer have a stomach!"

"Nor a functioning mouth," Davis said with a rueful smile, "I'll miss the sweet taste of wine and whisky!"

"And the taste of a girl's sweet lips!" Ferris added, "But you have had more than your fair share over the years!"

Davis sighed, "It only seems like yesterday that I was living the good life!"

"More like a debauched life you mean!" Ferris turned his collar up as they approached the group of onlookers.

"Do you notice anything odd about these people?" Davis asked quietly.

"If they are friends of yours, I would not be surprised how odd they are!"

"Their feet don't touch the ground!" Davis said, "Some are floating above the ground and some are definitely beneath the ground!"

"They must be friends of yours," Ferris snorted, "Mine wouldn't be that careless!" He looked at the feet, and sure enough, the children floated well above the ground. He walked around them to see if he could locate the means of suspension but none was apparent.

Some of the others were rooted deep in the grass and then he noticed one that had no feet to float or to be buried on.

Puzzled, he looked up at their faces and saw that there were different stages of mould on the skin, some green but mostly black. One or two of them sported a collection of white maggots crawling in what were the remains of the flesh.

"Brother mine," Ferris said in a whisper, "These must be your friends because they are all dead!"

"Not all mine!" Davis pointed to what was at one time a young woman, "Remember Ashley?"

"That cannot be Ashley," Ferris hissed, "I spoke to her a couple of months ago!"

"More like a couple of years; doesn't time fly!" Davis corrected his brother.

The one time woman's mouth opened, "Hello Ferris, Davis is correct; I died of a drug overdose." A maggot fell out of her mouth. Ferris stared hard; he remembered the wide generous lips in a suntanned face framed by straw coloured hair but none of that beauty was to be seen now. The fragrant perfume had been replaced by that of chemicals, damp earth, and the sweet smell of something rotting.

"Hello Grandpa!" A little voice piped up below his belt level. One of the small children was staring up at him, staring with blank misty eyes in a hollow face. "I'm Veronica and you passed me on the street after the car sped away." The small body was twisted and the head was stuck on at a strange angle, almost as an afterthought. "Why did you not stop and help me Grandpa?"

A rough almost skeletal hand was thrust at his shoulder, "Do you remember how I was left in a Turkish prison? You had the key in your hand and all you needed to do was insert it in the lock and turn it; instead you laughed and turned away."

Ferris shook his head as each of the visitors spoke of some misdeed. It was not that he did anything, just that he did nothing; he never extended the helping hand to these and many others, he could hear them all faintly calling from the distant past.

"Something is wrong here" Ferris groped for a handkerchief to wipe his face.

"Perhaps!" Davis took his arm in a fleshless grip, "or perhaps everything is finally as it should be!"

"What do you mean?" Ferris twisted to free himself, "You're dead, and you're all dead! How can I see and talk to you?"

It was difficult to tell if Davis was smiling without his lips, but there was an inflection in his voice that suggested that he was, "You are perfectly correct, brother mine; we are all dead!"

"I just said that!" Ferris yelled, "So how can I see you?"

"Do you remember coming here today? Was it by bus or car, or perhaps you walked." Suggested Davis.

Ferris shook his head and felt something wet trickle down his face, "I must have come by bus; what of it?"

Davis turned his brother round to face where the sextons were just finishing their task, "It is usual at a burial that the priest waits for all of the relatives to leave the graveside before giving the order to fill the grave; it is also usual for the priest to say a few comforting words to the bereaved. What did the priest say to you? Did he give comfort and reassurance for the life beyond?"

Ferris really felt uncomfortable, "I wasn't paying attention!"

"Shall we go and see why you have no recent memories?" Davis's pull on the arm was irresistible and they glided over the ground just as the sextons placed the headstone in position. Davis stood and pointed at the inscription,

HERE LIES FERRIS CHARTERS

BORN 14 JANUARY 1958

Ferris felt weak at the knees, "That is impossible! It is some sick joke!"

"You died two years before me," explained Davis, "it is only recently that your body was found and we could now bury you; that is why it has no date of your demise, we do not know when that was."

"What happened to me?"

"It is more important to know what will happen to you in the future," Davis pointed to a figure in the trees, "That is your future; with that person, your Lord and Master! That is what happens to people who do not care about others."

A moan escaped from Ferris' withered lips as the figure gestured that he should follow into the gathering mists.

THE END

FOOTSTEPS

It was late evening, and the air was fresh after a shower of rain. Feeling comfortable and relaxed after spending a few hours with my friends, I was looking forward to an hour in front of the fire, look at a TV programme or two, before retiring to bed.

The pace of my journey home was not hurried as I passed other late revellers on a similar journey to my own, not many and in groups from two to five, noisy and in good humour. I turned off the main road into the residential streets; these were quiet, the occupants in their warm beds long ago.

My footsteps resounded off the brick walls, and it was then that I heard the steps following me down the street, a tap-tap a few metres behind me. I turned to see who it was but the street, shining from the recent rain, was empty and the footsteps had stopped.

Surprised, I turned back to continue and the footsteps resumed, slightly out of sync with my own steps. When I slowed down or speeded up, the footsteps did the same. Perhaps it was an echo from the brick walls, the hesitation caused by the distance of the houses.

A feeling of uneasiness came over me; the street was empty apart from me and the invisible companion and anything could happen.

Finally, I turned into the street where I lived; the street lights seemed brighter and more welcoming, just a few more paces and I could enter my home and lock the door. As I climbed the steps, the footsteps were right behind me and I dare not look round; I was sweating with almost uncontrollable fear.

With a shaking hand, I inserted the key and looked up at the glass pane, and I saw in the reflection a shadowy someone standing behind me.

THE END

OLD SOLDIERS

The old man could be seen sitting on the veranda every morning, rocking back and forth, his old pipe jutting from his dry mouth like a cannon. The straw hat was pulled down almost over his faded eyes, invisible behind the tinted spectacles.

He would nod to every passer-by, adult and child, male or female. He was also known to talk to any passing dogs and cats and whistle at the birds. By his side was an old dog that may once have been a labrador; it lay with its head on its paws, the ears and nose twitching at every sign of something nearby, and occasionally it would open the rheumy eyes to survey the passing world.

At midday, as the sun became uncomfortably hot, the man and dog would rise and retreat into the cool shadows of the house. They would reappear as the sun sank and painted the sky red; these were the only times that anyone could talk to him and the first of the day was the paperboy. He would stop and wait while the old man read the headlines, sucking on a peppermint that was given to him by the old man. Then the old man would tell stories of yesteryear, and while he spoke in a horse whisper, the boy could see in his mind the people he spoke of, the houses and funny looking cars, all rushing to nowhere in particular.

The old man spoke of wars in distant lands; he told of losing friends as they fought people he was told were enemies. In time, the enemies became friends, and the friends became enemies, all very confusing to the boy. On occasional days, the old man would be visited by equally old men, comrades he called them, and sometimes he said survivors. They all spoke in that quiet rasping whisper, as though their voices were far away.

They would smoke cigarettes, cigars, or pipes held in gnarled rheumatic fingers as they talked, sipping home-made wine, Elderberry, Plum, or Carrot, occasionally supplemented with something boiled in a cellar or outhouse. They spoke of strange lands, and produced souvenirs of their adventures, laughing as they told and retold how it had come about.

As they told their tales, a group of interested people would gather to listen, sitting on the stoop or lawn, young people learning about history. The youths cooed and aarhed, especially at the stories became more imaginative. The stories carried on late in the evenings, until the old men stumped off down the path on their way home, some arm in arm and quietly singing some long forgotten ballad.

If anyone called them heroes, they would be silenced, reprimanded, censored by the old men. To them, it was the most thrilling part of their lives, young blood rushed with excitement as they withstood the blasts of cannon and inclement weather, eating cold food out of a can, if they were lucky.

They also told of romances with exotic women in those far off lands, girls with dark hair and complexions who spoke in strange tongues. They told of jewels found lying on the ground, disgorged from some long forgotten volcano, strange fruits and flowers, and animals that defy the imagination.

The newspaper boy paused one morning, the rocking chair was empty; there was no hound at its master's feet. The boy walked up the steps and with a hesitation, he knocked on the door. Hearing no answer, he went around the back of the house, and there lay the old man with the faithful hound waiting for the man to wake.

Whatever had happened, it was sudden; perhaps a heart attack or a stroke; the old man would not reminisce with his comrades again, at least not in this life, and one can imagine that now he had a new audience to tell his tales, and hear some new ones from those that went earlier.

THE END

THE PLAYGROUND
CHAPTER ONE
A NEW TERM

Behind St Botulph's Church in the village of Bishopmount, next to the cemetery, was Botulph's Primary School, and this was where Janet Philips was heading; her first day as the head of the school. She did not have to go far as the school-house was next to the church; it had been one of the church buildings a few centuries earlier.

She had been in residence for almost a month, sorting out her furniture, meeting the parents and the other villagers, and finally arranging the new term. She was full of ideas of how to stimulate the children's imagination and learning. A couple of children with their mothers were already there as she unlocked the doors. These she found were her assistants. The rest of the students arrived in dribs and drabs, most of them a little late.

The first part of the morning went fairly well, up until the children were taken outside to play. There was a tarmac area that had possibly been a tennis court at one time, and there was a grass area right next to the cemetery wall where there were a roundabout, a climbing frame, and some rocking horses on springs.

"Occasionally, a ball will end up amongst the grave stones, but I don't think that the residents will mind," Father Roland Thurber had walked quietly into the room; "I heard the children in the playground and assumed that you would be free. How is your first day?"

Janet had jumped in surprise, even emitting a little shriek, "Oh, you surprised me! So far, no disasters."

"I didn't mean to startle you, Roland Thurber," Thurber smiled, "I was wondering when you wanted me to give their religious studies."

"I wanted to get the rest of the lessons settled in, but we can do that any time," Janet was not very religious and had omitted to arrange any Bible classes.

"There is no hurry," Thurber said, "Heaven can wait, as they say!"

"I was surprised that the school was so close to the churchyard," Janet pointed at the wall, "I would think that it would disturb the children."

Thurber looked at the wall, "Not really, most of the occupants are relatives of the children and they appear to draw comfort that their families are so close. The school was donated by the church, not me personally, as I am not that old! It is still on church land."

"I was brought up in towns," Janet started to lay out some books, "and this is so rural; I am still getting used to meeting cattle on the roads."

"You'll find that living here is very different," Thurber nodded, "but it has its advantages; everything is at a slower pace making life most enjoyable."

"Do you hold a Harvest Festival?" Janet asked, "I do so love them!"

"Most certainly," Thurber said, "As this is a rural place, there is great emphasis on farming; I even bless the animals on *Saint* Francis' Day."

"All animals?" questioned Janet.

"We are all God's creatures!" Thurber smiled as he replied.

CHAPTER TWO

AN ABUSIVE CHILD

There was one small boy that Janet took to immediately, Bernard Troughton; he was small for his age and came from a poor family. His mother was single, and finding ends hard to meet; he was shy and withdrawn, and a target for other children of a spiteful nature.

The main antagonist was Shirley Barnes, a loud-mouthed mousey-haired girl who picked on Bernard all of the time. She possessed a foul vocabulary, which Janet found out was provided to her by her grandfather, a vile man in his dotage. Her parents did not try to control the old man.

To be fair, Shirley was abusive to everyone, and after several failed attempts to curb the girl's behaviour, Janet pretended not to hear, and spent her energies on stopping the other children from copying her. During any sporting event, Shirley would kick, punch and bite the other children; this brought the parents of the injured children in to school, and it soon became a tedious task to pacify those parents.

One day during a ball play, Janet noticed that some adults were standing in the cemetery and looking over the wall at the children; in all, there were about twenty of them. At first she was worried for the children's safety, but when the audience reappeared a few days later in an even greater number, Janet thought that they were there to prevent Shirley's and others misbehaviour. After that, Janet took no notice.

At the end of September, the villagers brought food and flowers from the fields and gardens to St Botulph's Church for the Harvest Festival. Being a rural area, the amount of produce from not just the fields, but the gardens and allotments as well. On the day before, the church looked more like a market with giant marrows, onions and potatoes, and the air held the perfume of thousands of flowers.

Little Bernard and his mother brought in some perfect tomatoes and Thurber made a special effort to praise the boy. "We grew them in the kitchen," said Bernard shyly.

"We do not all need farms to grow perfect crops," Thurber patted the boy's head.

Janet was standing nearby and noticed Shirley glaring at the boy and priest. She had never seen such an evil expression on anyone's face before and that worried her; she had a foreboding that something bad would happen.

The following day, something bad did happen. The church was opened early for the Harvest Festival, and Thurber went out briefly; on his return, he saw Shirley smashing Bernard's tomatoes. For an instant, he felt like lashing out at the miscreant but at the last moment, he just grabbed her shoulder.

Shirley whirled round and Thurber gasped, let go of her shoulder and stepped back. The face he saw did not belong to a human being; it was so twisted and contorted and made worse by the red tomato juice that was splashed there. Now that she was released, the girl ran past the priest and out of the door.

Thurber stood immobile, his face ashen and he was still like that when Janet arrived with a bunch of flowers. For a moment, he looked past the teacher into a different landscape, and then he refocussed.

"I think that I have just seen Lilith!"

Janet frowned, "I've just seen Shirley run out; who is Lilith?"

The expression on Thurber's face was one of fear and confusion, "In all of my years of service, I have never seen such an evil thing, or heard of anyone who has; Lilith is the snake in the Garden of Eden!"

Janet looked hard at the priest and almost thought of smelling his breath for alcohol, "You will have to explain."

Thurber smiled and took her arm, "It is an alternative version of the Book of Genesis, and Man's fall from grace. It is one of the oldest texts in the world, and describes Lilith as the first wife of Adam, before Eve. Adam and Lilith were made from the same red mud, but Lilith would not be subservient to the man and laid with a demon or an archangel called Shamael, who would develop into Shatan or as you would call him Satan. She is totally evil, and I have just seen Lilith's countenance in the face of Shirley. Or was it Shirley?"

"She is a difficult child," Janet agreed, "but surely you cannot consider her to be like this creature Lilith; that thing is just a myth!"

"And so I thought before today," Thurber sat on a pew, "Let me rest a moment and think this through."

Janet sat next to him, worried that the old man was suffering from something like a stroke.

After some minutes of playing with the rosary, he looked up, "I will have to look at this later, in the meantime would you help me to clean up this mess that Shirley made?" he pointed to the smashed tomatoes.

"Oh, that's Bernard's!" Janet exclaimed, "I have some tomatoes at home and I will replace them. What a wicked girl!" Then she remembered the expression on the girl's face the day before, "You could be right about her being a bad girl, but a devil, even the Devil!"

"In my life I have seen some remarkable things, some good and some bad, but I have never seen such evil in anyone's face before," Thurber went to fetch some cleaning materials.

CHAPTER THREE

THURBER REVEALS

Nothing else happened; Shirley appeared for the festival looking as innocent as a babe, and Thurber avoided looking at her. Janet on the other hand, stood at the back of the hall and watched her carefully. She continued watching her every school day until the end of October, then it was Halloween, when all of the dead came out of the graves, and demons abound.

Janet entered into the Spirit of Trick or Treat without associating anything with it; the children drew masks and made up costumes, some of them obviously 'encouraged' by their parents, and the school walls were decorated with pictures of flying witches and black cats. Everyone except Shirley.

That stumped Janet, as she thought that it would have been the ideal opportunity to cause some mayhem. She was just packing up the school at the end of the day, when Thurber poked his head round the door.

"Just the person I want to see!" Janet exclaimed.

"I wish all my parishioners thought the same way," Thurber sat on one of the small tables.

"It's about Shirley," Janet began and saw a shadow pass over the priest's face, "She does not join in anything! Today we were preparing for Halloween, and she did nothing but sulk! I think that this antisocial behaviour is something to do with her overall attitude."

"In part, you are correct," Thurber looked uneasy, "This is far more serious than that! You have no doubt noticed her bad language," Janet nodded, "It is her grandfather who has done that, but also he has an even greater influence in other areas. I have thought that he is now a bit ga-ga, senile, but it appears he is as bright as a pin, although a very dark one."

"I don't understand," Janet had stopped tidying.

"I was in town talking with a very old priest, even older that I; I brought up the question of Shirley and her grandfather and he said that I should look around the cemetery walls. That's all he said, and so I have. On the far side, there is a plaque placed in the wall, I do not understand why I have never seen it before, it simply said that Jerimiah Judas Barnes was buried outside of consecrated ground on the 17th January 1649. Her grandfather's name is Jeremiah Judas!"

"Why outside?" Janet asked.

"Usually because they were considered evil, such as vampires and witches." Thurber said.

"Well, it cannot be the same Jeremiah, he is just bones now!" Janet said.

"Ah, I took it a bit further," Thurber really looked terrible, "I found out what his crime was, he was a disciple of Satan and he ran a coven inside the church. There was a period when the church was not in use due to the Civil War, and Barnes took it over for his own ends."

Janet gave a short laugh, "You don't believe in that rubbish, do you?"

Thurber look up at her, "I am a servant of God, I believe in the goodness of Heaven and God, and there is always an opposite and equal force which we call

Satan, Hell, the Devil, and that I believe also. God or Mother Nature, call it what you will, always balances everything."

Janet sat stunned for some long moments, "If that is true, it would explain many things, such as the expression I saw on her face before the Harvest Festival."

Thurber nodded, "I saw a frightful visage when she was destroying those tomatoes. It is only a small thing that she did, but she is still young and her hatred or powers will increase."

"That Barnes was a long time ago, so what is the connection?" Janet asked.

"I cannot find a birth or death for a male Barnes since that date!" Thurber wrung his hands, "I fear that he is not buried, or at least some of him is still in this life."

"Perhaps they were born and died somewhere else," Janet suggested.

"The records show that the family always lived here," Thurber's eyes were full of tears, "I do not know if we can correct the history and remove the threat."

"Are you telling me that we have a diabolical evil in the village," Janet asked, "or just some lunatic?"

"Either would be unwanted," moaned Thurber, "but I fear that it is most probably the former!"

CHAPTER FOUR

HALLOWEENS

Despite Thurber's fears, Halloween went off fairly smoothly; the younger children came to the houses with their parents who had to remind them what to say, and the older children came in gangs of about four or five, laughing and joking as teenagers do.

Janet was tense when the evening started, but as time passed, she relaxed until about nine o'clock when the last Trick or Treater went home with their treasure. Peace at last settled on Bishopmount and Janet decided to read a book, a historical fiction novel about the War of the Roses.

She read a chapter, and then decided to shower and then make some hot chocolate. She sat curled up on the sofa sipping the drink and started to think about Thurber's theory. To her, it was obvious that there were missing records to explain the missing births and deaths; how can anyone live for three hundred years. It was nonsensical!

Then she remembered the Biblical Methuselah who had supposed to have lived for nine hundred years. What if that was true, what if in ancient times people could live for an extremely long time, and could it be possible that some still could? She shivered at the thought, and then smiled when she remembered Sammy Davis Junior singing that no one would want a nine hundred year old guy. With that happier thought, she went to bed.

Later she woke up, it was still dark and she was fuzzy from waking from a sound sleep. Was that someone knocking on the door, or was it someone else's door. She staggered to the window and had to look twice at the scene below.

In the playground, the roundabout was merrily spinning and the rocking horses were whipping back and forth making the knocking noise, but there was no one near them! Then she became aware that beyond the wall there were the people who watched the children. They were bathed in a greenish glow and there were far more than she had seen previously.

As her head cleared, the details became clearer; she always thought that they were poorly dressed but some of these were naked or just dressed in a white sheet. Then she saw that one or two were just skeletons with hardly any flesh on the bones.

She tried to think of a rational reason and thought that this was some adult Halloween thing, performed long after the children were asleep. She looked at her clock and her heart almost stopped; it read midnight, the Witching Hour!

CHAPTER FIVE

THE STANDING WATCHERS

Janet sat up all night with the lights on. As soon as it was light enough, she dressed and went directly to the rectory and rang the bell several times before Thurber opened the door.

He took one look at her face and opened the door wider, "What is it child? Come in!"

They went to the kitchen where Thurber put the kettle on, but he produced a bottle of whiskey and two glasses; in his estimation, she was in shock and the drink would restore the colour in her dead white face. Janet downed the drink in one go with a shudder.

"Father, do you really believe in the supernatural?" she asked.

"God is a supernatural being, something more than mankind," he replied, "so I do believe, but you're talking about the black side, the ghosts and things."

Janet nodded vigorously, "At midnight exactly, I saw the dead rise from the graves out there!"

Thurber looked at the window and blinked, "Are you sure that it wasn't a bad dream?"

"A day ago, I didn't believe, and now you don't believe me!" Janet cried.

"I was just checking for alternative reasons, after all, we were celebrating Halloween and we had that discussion," Thurber tried to calm her, "perhaps all of that could have caused a nightmare."

Janet shook her head, "It was the group that comes and watches the children play, plus some others."

"What group?" Thurber frowned, "This is the first I have heard about anyone watching the children."

"They stand by the wall on the church side," Janet sobbed, "I thought that they were parents, but now I realise that it was the children's dead relatives."

Thurber sat back in his chair, "Have the children seen them, said anything?"

Janet shook her head.

"Do you mind if I look after the school today?" Thurber asked, "It will give me an excuse to look around. This is most disturbing! You had better stay at home and rest."

"Oh no!" Janet said, "I do not want to be alone!"

"Very well! I will get dressed and we will have some breakfast. I do not believe that whiskey is the way to start the day!" said Thurber.

Together, they had breakfast by which time Janet had calmed down, and then they walked to the school.

"They were standing there," Janet pointed to a spot on the wall, "They are always standing there."

"Do you see them arrive or leave?" the priest asked.

"No I don't," Janet pulled her lip, "I never thought of that; they are just there when I look and then they are gone."

"Only when the children are playing?" Thurber asked.

"I don't know," said Janet, "I never look for them when I am inside."

Thurber scratched his chin, "I do not understand what is going on!"

"What do you mean?"

"There must be a reason for them to appear, and I cannot see it!" said Thurber, "You carry on and I will poke around."

Thurber walked the length of the stone wall, occasionally bending down to look at something, and then he walked back on the other side. Stopping in thought for a while, or was it prayer, he looked at the grave stones, reading the names and dates. He found a few of the Barnes women but no male Barnes.

The children appeared on the playing field, and Thurber talked to some of them.

"Have you seen anyone looking over this wall when you play?" he asked each of them the same question. The answer was a negative shake of the head, but some of them looked doubtful. He stood back and watched them for a while, and then he felt someone tugging on his sleeve; it was little Bernard Troughton.

"Please sir, what did you mean?"

"I just wondered if you had seen anyone there," Thurber explained.

"Do you mean Uncle Tom?" Bernard asked.

"Who is Uncle Tom?"

"He isn't really an uncle," The boys face screwed up, "he used to help Mum now and then, but he disappeared about two years ago."

Thurber's blood ran cold, "Do you see Uncle Tom looking over the wall?"

Bernard nodded, "And sometimes he brings his friends!"

The priest felt nauseated and sat on the wall before his legs collapsed, "Have any of the other children seen Uncle Tom and his friends?"

Bernard pointed to a boy next to him, "Charley sees his cousin, don't you?" The boy nodded.

Other children came up and announced to the astonished priest that they had seen 'people' at the wall.

Thurber almost ran from the playground to the church where he took a large whiskey before praying for guidance. Later, he rang the bishop for a long and serious discussion.

CHAPTER SIX

JERIMIAH JUDAS BARNES

The first thought that Thurber had was not to alarm anyone in the village, but Janet sought him out and asked if he had found anything.

"Well, it seems that I am the last to know that something was happening in my church!" He rubbed his thinning hair, "Most of the children have seen the 'Watchers', and that they recognised them as dead relatives."

"Why didn't they say anything?" Janet asked.

"Consider the very young," Thurber explained, "Everything in their world is new, and every day there is something to learn; as we adults never said anything, because we didn't see them, so the children accepted the 'Watchers' as normal, not knowing that adults had a form of blindness."

Janet shuddered, "But why are they watching?"

"That is the real question," Thurber said, "Everything has a reason, and we just have to find out. The accepted theory for spirits to hang about is that they are troubled, so what is troubling them?"

"Barnes, Jerimiah Judas Barnes!" Janet exclaimed, "He is the reason, and Shirley as well!"

Thurber looked surprised, "You could be right! They are the only really bad disturbance in the village, but what is Barnes ultimate goal, what does he want to do?"

"What do we know about his life, I mean the original Barnes?" Janet asked.

"I have some records in the church," Thurber said, "When you finish for the day, come round to the vicarage and we can go through them."

"I am ready now!" Janet said, "Lead on!"

In Thurber's study, was a closet that was full of papers, some in boxes and others in loose bundles. Talking to himself, he sorted through them, blowing dust as he went.

"It is a long time since I looked in here, they were all written by my predecessors, and their handwriting is terrible." He pulled one box out and peered at the label, "Ah, this is the one I think, 1645 to 1661."

He placed it on his desk, "I will make a pot of coffee, for I fear that it will take some time; meanwhile, you can start but be careful, some of the pages are delicate."

When Thurber returned with coffee and biscuits, Janet was frowning at a page, "You were understating about the handwriting, this is terrible!"

Thurber looked over her shoulder, "Archibald Fremond, unfortunately, he wrote more than anyone else!" He took a few pages and sat in the armchair.

An hour later, Janet gasped and Thurber looked round, "What is it?"

"Here is what Barnes was doing," Janet was excitedly shaking a paper, "There are several pages."

Thurber went to the desk and read the almost unintelligible writing, then he took the second page and then the third, "Well, well, he was a bad one alright!"

"Some of the words I do not know," Janet said.

"I am not surprised!" Thurber answered, "There are terms here that relate to heathenism, barbaric practices."

"Oh my God!" Janet's hands were trembling, "He was executed by fire!"

Thurber took the page and read it for himself, "He was first hung and then faggots were placed under him, but during all of this, he was conscious and talking!"

"Can a person talk when they are being hung?" Janet asked.

With a shake of his head, Thurber answered in the negative, "If it was a quick execution when the neck snaps, the victim has no control, and if it is a slow one, he strangles and has no air to talk."

"It is a horrible way to die!" Janet pulled a face.

"It was ordered by the church, our scribbly friend Archibald Fremond, not by a court of law," Thurber went back to what he was reading originally.

"Was it legal?" Janet asked.

"That is a very good question," Thurber mumbled as he read, "Even the church would hold some sort of hearing and place judgement, and I can see nothing here about a court of any sort."

"Was it the vigilantes that killed him?"

"I am beginning to suspect that it was," Thurber said, "Barnes had taken some of the young women of the village, most of them according to this, and started a cult where he had carnal knowledge and produced several children. Two of the girls were related to…"

"Archibald Fremond," Janet finished the sentence, "Here is a list of those girls, and two of them were Fremond twins! It was an act of revenge against Barnes!"

"According to this, when the bonfire was over, nothing remained of Barnes." Thurber held up the paper, "and that is impossible, a bonfire does not burn everything, especially the bones; it is not hot enough!"

Janet appeared not to have heard him; she was reading the list she had found, "Do you realise that the names of these girls are the same as most of them in the school?"

Thurber leaned back in his chair, "I always thought that it was strange that there were no new families in the village for a long time. That explains it!"

"Does it also mean that the current villagers could see the forbears all along and just kept Mum?" Janet felt the hair stand up on her arms.

Janet felt quite nervous on the following day, trying to appear normal but looking at people and wondering if her suspicions were real. Even little Bernard appeared to her in a different light, but after a few hours of activity with the children, she lost that feeling of dread – almost.

When she called in at the store, meeting the other adults brought the feeling back stronger than ever, especially the store owner, George Sommers and his wife who kept looking at her in a strange way. With a shake of her head, Janet pulled herself together and told herself not to be so foolish.

Thurber was under pressure all night; he spoke to the archbishop of his discoveries and fears for a long time. The Bishop and he were old friends, so the conversation was informal.

"You must be mistaken Rolly," the Bishop said, "these things only happen in those horror films that are such a fad these days."

"Bob, I tell you that everything that I have just said is true," Thurber insisted, "the young woman will back up everything; I am sure that this Barnes fellow has lived since the Civil War!"

"I don't know what to say to you," Bishop Robert Murphy was troubled, "I know that you are sincere in this belief, but this is not the Middle Ages and we do not believe in such things."

"We still believe in evil, or at least I do," Thurber said, "We need to perform a special exorcism to rid us of this creature and its offspring."

There was a short silence, "Rolly, that would include most if not all of the villagers; have you given any thought as to how you could do this, and the publicity if news got out?"

"I can start with protecting the boundary, and then hold a normal mass." Thurber sounded dejected, "I was hoping that it would be 'we' that do this, but I hear that you are holding back."

"Are you sure of your facts?" Murphy asked, "after all, you are basing your argument on what could be a clerical error."

"I can find the records of everyone else except this one," Thurber said earnestly, "if I have those, how can the record miss this one who also displays a corrupting influence?"

There was a long sigh, "I will come down and see things for myself, but if I find that you are getting senile and that there could be an alternative explanation, I will have to think about replacing you!"

"And the young woman, how will you deal with her," Thurber asked, "and all the children who also claim to have seen these 'watchers'?"

"I will come down tomorrow Rolly," Murphy said, "Warn the young woman of my arrival and why I am coming."

CHAPTER EIGHT

THE MASS

Janet met the Bishop, and explained about the 'watchers' that she and the children had seen. He made her describe in more detail how the 'watchers' appeared, their dress and behaviour. He listened intently as she described how the children acted when the admitted to seeing their dead relatives.

"Thank you Miss Philips, you can carry on for now, but I may wish to talk to the children later," Murphy turned to Thurber, "Now Rolly, let us examine your records."

After about two hours of going over records several times, Murphy leaned back and rubbed his eyes, "I cannot fault your investigation, not that I expected to do so, but absence of the record does not prove your point. Have you met this Barnes?"

Thurber shook his head, "Never seen him in all the time I have lived in the village, but his so-called granddaughter is in Janet's school; she is a vile handful and you can see her for yourself right now."

The children were in the playground, and the two clerics stood looking at them for a while. When Janet saw them, she looked surprised.

I thought that you were the 'watchers' for a moment," she explained.

Murphy smiled, "In a sense were are, we are watching the children; which is this granddaughter of Barnes?"

Janet pointed out Shirley, and they watched as she shouted at another child, using the worst language possible. Then she pounced on another child and placed him in a headlock.

"She is like this all of the time," Janet said.

"She has a remarkable command of the vulgar language," Murphy noted.

"That is due to her grandfather," Janet winced as Shirley let loose another cannonade of foul language, "I cannot stop her!"

"What are her parents like?" asked Murphy.

"I have only met the mother, and she is a timid, mousey person," Janet said, "The father has never been near the school."

Murphy said nothing, but gave a tiny nod as he continued watching the children. The children finished playing and went in with Janet; Thurber and Murphy went back to the vicarage.

"I think that we can perform a mass on Sunday morning, just a normal one so that I can judge the people," Murphy said.

Early on Sunday morning, Thurber and Murphy started to arrange the church for the mass, while Janet decided to lay out the school for the following week. There was a knocking noise, a regular thump – thump, and then it was joined my something else, and then another.

Janet looked out of the window and her heart stopped! The whole playground was in motion; the carousel was whirling like a top, and the swings were swinging like maniacs, and the animal-rides were frantically nodding; and nobody was in sight to make them do this!

She dropped the books she was holding and backed slowly away from the window. She turned and ran out of the school and headed towards the open doors of the church and into the arms of Bishop Murphy.

"Whoa Janet, you'll break something . . ." then he noticed that her face was white and she had been crying, "What is wrong? Why are you running?"

Janet was gasping for air and just pointed towards the school. As he stood on the steps of St Botulph's he could see that everything was madly spinning and nodding.

Thurber came to the door, "What's ...", and then he saw the manic playground and his jaw dropped.

"Come inside!" Murphy took Janet's hand and pulled her inside, and then he turned and pulled Thurber inside as he swung the heavy door shut. "I do not know what is happening, but we are safer here."

The Bishop paused with his fingers on his lip, "The best thing for now is to pray to the Lord Almighty," and with that, he stepped towards the altar and the other two followed. While they prayed, they could still hear the playground equipment going mad.

Thurber kept looking round as though expecting the animated toys to come bouncing through the door, and after a while, he noticed a green reflection in the shiny surface of the cross. Puzzled, he looked round, stopped praying, and nudged the Bishop. Murphy looked behind them and his eyes bulged.

The pews behind them were filled with the ranks of the 'Watchers', standing quietly in their ragged and soiled clothes and bathed in a pale green light. Janet let out a scream, and Thurber almost joined her.

As they stood frozen in front of the altar, the large wooden doors swung open and the church was filled with a nauseating stench. Hurriedly, the three covered their noses and mouths, although that made little difference.

Through the doors came an amazing figure; at first it looked like it had four legs, but then the second pair of legs separated to become a smaller version of the main figure. Janet moaned, as it resembled Shirley Barnes and that meant that the main figure must be Jerimiah Judas Barnes, a nightmare figure.

The face was white and scarred, as though it was covered in old and fresh boils; he walked like a crab, dragging one foot behind, but the worst thing was the expression in his eyes. Thurber had never seen such deathly hatred, and the focus was on them.

The Bishop took his cross from his neck and held it forward, but Thurber reached round and seized the large gold cross from the altar and using it as a shield, he stepped quickly towards Barnes, so quickly that the cross smashed into the monstrous head.

Instantly, the ghostly congregation disappeared as Barnes reeled back with a scream that ended with a cough, or was it a curse. Shirley was caught in her grandfather's long coat as Barnes senior flew backwards out of the doors. This allowed the coat to fly open to reveal a large serpent's body where a man's should be. The stench followed them out as the doors slammed shut.

"W – What was that?" Janet asked in a shaky voice.

"I do not think that I want to know!" Thurber replaced the cross and noting that a corner had melted where it met the monster's head.

"Well done Rolly," Murphy said, his voice was unsteady, "Obviously, my small cross was not powerful enough."

"I think that hitting it was what caused it to back out," Thurber sounded calm but his hands shook.

"What was it?" Janet asked again.

"A demon" Thurber said, "the first that I have ever seen! I surmise that at some time in the past it took over Jerimiah Judas Barnes' body and has continued to exist in that way."

"In the Book of Enoch, it tells of angels falling to earth and consorting with mortal women," the Bishop said thoughtfully, "if that is true, then the girl is his offspring."

"The Book of Enoch is not a part of the Bible," Thurber explained to Janet, "When they were compiling what we call the Bible today, certain texts were left out and Enoch is one of those."

"I thought that the Bible was all that there was!" Janet said.

Bishop Murphy continued, "Have you heard of the Dead Sea Scrolls?" Janet nodded, "Those are copies of the books that were discarded. The script goes back to before there was writing, and first appeared in a land called Sumer where writing was first practiced."

"The stories are from heathens that practiced a different religion to our own," Thurber added, "such as the Biblical Flood."

"So was there a flood?" Janet asked, wide eyed.

"Oh yes," Thurber nodded, "several in fact; we know that from the science of geology."

"You see, the Bible was copied from the Jewish Torah, and they collected all of the stories from cultures going back a long time, perhaps hundreds of thousands of years, so there is a basis of truth there but it has been distorted over time."

"The important thing is that we adhere to the Gospels, and remain God-fearing!" Thurber ended the explanation.

"What has just happened?" Janet asked, "Where does that fit in with what you are saying?"

"We are not sure," Murphy said, "it will take time to sort that out, but Barnes was a demon that took over a whole family."

"Well, thank God that is all over with!" Janet sighed.

CHAPTER NINE

THE END?

"Do you think that it was wise to tell her?" Murphy said.

"We had to tell her something," Thurber answered, "but although she thinks that it is over, it is not! Demons have been around since the dawn of time, and this was just a skirmish, not even a battle in a long war."

"Will the Watchers come back do you think?"

Thurber shrugged, "Maybe, but we have contained that one that we can call Barnes, I am sure. In a few days, when the shock has worn off, Janet will start thinking of questions, so I ask myself, how much should I tell her?"

"As little as possible, I would advise," Murphy rose and shook Thurber's hand, "If the population knew the whole truth, there would be a mass panic!"

THE END

ABOUT THE AUTHORS

Danny White and Mike Williamson are members of an artistic family, a large one, but it is only recently that they got together on a book. Danny read the first chapter of Mike's supernatural book 'OLD CHURCH' and was so fired by the description, that he had to paint a picture that is now the cover of the book.

More recently, he painted a picture of a young woman and added a wolf and the moon. While painting it, he came up with a story behind the picture and this became 'LUBIN', the title story of this collection of short stories and the picture is the front cover.

Both Danny and Mike live in the County of Essex, although forty miles apart.

Printed in Great Britain
by Amazon